The Princess
The Hockey Player
Magic and
Ghosts

The Princess
The Hockey Player
Magic and
Ghosts

Edited by Muriel Whitaker
Illustrated by
Vlasta van Kampen

Hurtig Publishers
Edmonton

Copyright © 1980 by Hurtig Publishers Ltd.

Hurtig Publishers Ltd.
10560 – 105 Street
Edmonton, Alberta

Canadian Cataloguing in Publication Data

Main entry under title:

The Princess, the hockey player, magic & ghosts

ISBN 0-88830-194-4

1. Children's stories, Canadian (English).*
I. Whitaker, Muriel, 1923-   II. Van Kampen, Vlasta.
PS8321.P75   jC813'.01089282   C81-091182-5
PZ5.P75

Printed and bound in Canada
by T. H. Best Printing Company Limited

Contents

The Princess of Tomboso / *Marius Barbeau
  and Michael Hornyansky* / 9
Ko-ishin-mit Goes Fishing / *George Clutesi* / 25
The Man Whose Soul Could Travel / *Peter Lum* / 30
How Old Paul Invented Doughnuts / *Gloria Logan* / 37
A Daughter of Eve / *L. M. Montgomery* / 43
Fog Magic / *Julia L. Sauer* / 54
The Bobolink / *Duncan Campbell Scott* / 67
A Child in Prison Camp / *Shizuye Takashima* / 73
Knowing Anna / *D. P. Barnhouse* / 79
How the Crow Boy Forms His Magic / *Donald Suddaby* / 86
The Adventure of Billy Topsail / *Norman Duncan* / 109
Little Baptiste / *E. W. Thomson* / 119
Series Jitters / *Leslie McFarlane* / 134
Buggam Grange: A Good Old Ghost Story /
  Stephen Leacock / 148

Acknowledgements

The editor wishes to thank the following for permission to include in this anthology previously copyrighted material:

"The Princess of Tomboso" from *The Golden Phoenix* by Marius Barbeau, retold by Michael Hornyansky, reprinted by permission of Oxford University Press.

"Ko-ishin-mit Goes Fishing" from *Son of Raven, Son of Deer* by George Clutesi, reprinted by permission of Gray's Publishing Limited.

"How Old Paul Invented Doughnuts" by Gloria Logan from *Rubaboo 2*, reprinted by permission of Gage Publishing Limited.

"A Daughter of Eve" from *Emily of New Moon* by L. M. Montgomery, reprinted by permission of The Canadian Publishers, McClelland and Stewart Limited, Toronto.

"Fog Magic" from *Fog Magic* by Julia L. Sauer. Copyright © 1943 by Julia L. Sauer, copyright © renewed 1971 by Julia L. Sauer. Reprinted by permission of Viking Penguin Inc.

"The Bobolink" from *In the Village of Viger* by Duncan Campbell Scott, reprinted by permission of John G. Aylen, Ottawa.

6

"A Child in Prison Camp" from *A Child in Prison Camp* by Shizuye Takashima, reprinted by permission of Tundra Books of Montreal.

"Knowing Anna" by D. P. Barnhouse, reprinted by permission of the author.

"How the Crow Boy Forms His Magic" from *The Moon of Snowshoes* by Donald Suddaby, reprinted by permission of Oxford University Press.

"Series Jitters" from *Breakaway* by Leslie McFarlane, reprinted by permission of Methuen Publications.

"Buggam Grange: A Good Old Ghost Story" from *Winnowed Wisdom* by Stephen Leacock, reprinted by permission of The Canadian Publishers, McClelland and Stewart Limited, Toronto.

While every effort has been made to trace the owners of copyrighted material and to make due acknowledgement, the editor regrets having been unsuccessful with the following selection: "The Man Whose Soul Could Travel" by Peter Lum.

For Bernadette and Adam
and other grandchildren
to come

The Princess of Tomboso

Marius Barbeau and Michael Hornyansky

There was once a king who had three sons. They did none of the things that princes are supposed to do, but stayed at home all day and ate their father out of house and home. When the old king lay dying, he called them to his bedside and said:

"My children, I have only one thing left to give you when I die. It is an old bowl. When you have buried me, go to the barn and you will find it behind the door. Pick it up and shake it, each of you in turn. Whatever falls out of it is your inheritance."

Then the old man breathed his last.

It was the custom in those days to keep the dead lying in state for a day and a night; but the king's sons were so anxious to see what the bowl held that they buried their father without delay. Then they ran to the barn and looked behind the door. Sure enough, the bowl was there.

The eldest son picked it up and shook it well. Presto! A silk purse fell into the air. Written on it in letters of gold were these words:

Every time I open wide
a hundred florins are inside.

He opened the purse wide, and — *cling, clang!* — a hundred shining florins tumbled to the ground. He closed the purse, opened it wide again, and found it still full to the brim.

"It works!" he exclaimed. "I'm rich!"

The second brother was growing impatient.

"Now it's my turn," he said.

He took the bowl, held it over his head, and shook it. This time a silver bugle fell out. Written on it in letters of gold were these words:

> *Blow one end, and your troops appear;*
> *the other, and the field is clear.*

The second prince lost no time. Putting the bugle to his lips, he blew a short blast. *Ta-rraa!* There in the field behind the barn stood an army of ten thousand soldiers waiting for his command.

Then he put the wide end of the bugle to his lips and blew again. Presto! In a twinkling the field was empty.

"It works!" he exclaimed. "I'm powerful!"

"Now it's my turn," said the youngest brother, whose name was Jacques.

He took the bowl and shook it. A leather belt fell out. Written on it in letters of gold were these words:

> *Put me on and tell me where:*
> *quick as lightning you'll be there.*

Jacques lost no time. Clasping the belt around his waist, he wished himself into the castle. *Whoosh!* — and there he stood inside the castle. He wished himself back into the barn. *Whoosh!* There he was back again.

"Well, it works," he said. "Now I can travel cheap."

"And just where do you propose to go?" asked his eldest brother.

"To Tomboso," said Jacques promptly. "With my belt it will be a simple thing to visit the Princess."

His brothers looked jealous. They had heard of the Princess of Tomboso, who was as beautiful as the moon. But they had never seen her, and they didn't have a magic belt.

"You'd better look out," they told him. "She'll play some trick on you."

"Oh, no fear of that."

"Anyway, the royal guards won't even let you into the castle."

"The guards won't trouble me," said Jacques. "I'll just wish myself into the Princess's chamber, and *whoosh!* I'll be there. Farewell, my brothers."

Clasping the belt around him, he made his wish. *Whoosh!* There he stood, in the finest room he had ever seen. And sitting on a velvet cushion by the window, eating a red apple, was the Princess of Tomboso, as beautiful as the moon.

When the Princess saw a man in her room, she gave a faint scream.

"Fair Princess," Jacques began, "do not be alarmed."

But it was too late. The Princess had fainted. Jacques sprang forward and caught her in his arms. He gazed at her in admiration. Never in his life had he seen such a lovely creature.

Presently the Princess opened her eyes.

"Are you a man from this world," she asked, "or an angel from heaven?"

"Princess, I'm a real man."

She sat up. "Then how did you arrive in my chamber? The doors are guarded, and the windows are high above the ground."

Jacques smiled modestly. "Ah, Princess, for me it was very

simple. Do you see this belt I'm wearing? Well, it's no ordinary belt. I wished myself into your chamber, and *whoosh!* It brought me here."

"A magic belt? That's quite impossible," declared the Princess. "I don't believe you."

"Sweet Princess, you have something to learn. Watch me."

He wished himself down into the castle courtyard. *Whoosh!* There he was. The Princess stared down at him from her window. Then he wished himself back into her room and landed at the foot of the bed. The Princess was struck dumb with amazement.

"There," he said. "Now do you believe me?"

"What is your name?" asked the Princess.

"They call me Jacques."

"Well, Jacques, I think you are the most outrageous liar I've ever met."

"Princess, I have told you the plain truth."

She bit her lip in thought. "Perhaps it is true for you," she said. "But would it work for me too?"

"Certainly," said Jacques.

"Prove it, then. Let me see this marvelous belt of yours."

Jacques took off the belt and showed it to her. She read the words written in letters of gold: "*Put me on and tell me where: quick as lightning you'll be there.* Oh, Jacques!" she cried. "Lend it to me!"

"That I cannot do," he said firmly.

"Dear Jacques! *Please.*" And she held her arms out to him imploringly.

She looked so beautiful standing there before him that Jacques forgot his brothers' warning. He gave her the belt and watched her clasp it around her tiny waist.

"Now," she said, "I wish to be in my father's office."

12   Marius Barbeau and Michael Hornyansky

Whoosh! — and there she stood, in her father's office. The king was startled, but she gave him no explanation.

"Father!" she cried. "There is a rascal in my chamber!"

At once the king sent his guard of honour to her room. Forty soldiers seized hold of Jacques and gave him a thorough beating. When he seemed half dead, they opened a window and threw him out of the castle.

Poor Jacques landed in the ditch by the roadside and lay there unconscious for three days and nights. When at last he came to his senses, he thought:

"I cannot go home now. When my brothers hear what has happened, they will finish me off."

But he had eaten nothing for days. He was starving.

"Ah, well," he said. "If I'm going to die, I might as well die at home."

When his brothers saw him stumbling up the path that evening, they knew that something must have happened to his belt. They came out of the castle shaking their fists, warning him what to expect if he came near.

But Jacques was too exhausted to care. He plodded into the castle while his brothers heaped reproaches and ridicule on his head.

"We ought to lock you up for the rest of your life," they said. "You can't be trusted on your own. Get in there under the stairs. We won't have anything more to do with you!"

For a whole month they kept him there, giving him nothing but bread and water. But one day Jacques said to his eldest brother:

"If you would lend me your purse, I could go and buy back my belt."

His brother sneered. "Do you think I would trust you with my purse after what happened to your belt?"

"But listen to my plan," said Jacques eagerly. "I'll go back to Tomboso and ask to speak to the Princess. When she asks what I want, I'll tell her the truth — that I want to buy back my belt. If she says I cannot pay for it, I shall open the purse wide and send a hundred florins rolling on the floor, *cling, clang!* If she wants more, I can fill her whole room with florins, right up to the ceiling. It won't cost you anything, for the purse is never empty. In the end I'll get my belt back."

His brother grumbled, but finally he agreed.

"But I warn you," he said, "if you come back without the purse, don't expect any mercy from me."

"No fear of that," said Jacques confidently.

And so he took the purse and made his way back to Tomboso. He asked to see the Princess. When she heard who it was, she had him shown up to her room. He found her eating a red apple and smiling.

"Why, hello, Jacques! And what can I do for you this fine day?"

"Fair Princess, I have come to buy back my belt."

"Your belt?" The Princess pretended not to understand. "My dear Jacques, what belt are you talking about?"

"Princess, I'll pay you a good price for it."

She laughed. "A young lad like you couldn't possibly afford to buy a valuable belt."

"I can fill this room with pieces of gold," said Jacques.

"How you boast, Jacques! Why, even my father the king hasn't enough gold florins to fill this room."

"I can fill it to the ceiling," said Jacques. "For me it's no trick at all."

The Princess shook her head. "Ah, Jacques, you never change. One simply can't believe a word you say."

"Very well, you shall see," said Jacques. "I have a little silk purse in my pocket. Open it wide, and a hundred florins tumble out. Open it wide again, and there are a hundred more."

He took the purse from his pocket and opened it wide, and — *cling, clang!* — a hundred shining florins fell to the floor. The Princess stared at them with round eyes.

"There," he said. "Now do you believe me?"

"Ah," she breathed. "With a purse like that, you can buy back any belt you like. But how can I be sure it will go on giving florins?"

"Look," said Jacques, "it's still full."

And — *cling, clang!* — he spilled another hundred gold pieces on the floor.

"Oh!" said the Princess. "Would it do that for me, too?"

"Certainly."

"Please let me try!"

"That I cannot do," said Jacques firmly.

"Dear Jacques! *Please.*" And she held out her arms as if to embrace him. She looked so beautiful that he forgot his resolutions and gave her the purse.

But she was still wearing the magic belt. At once she wished herself into her father's office. *Whoosh!*

The king looked up from his desk. "Terrible draught in here," he said. "Oh, it's you, my dear. What's the matter now?"

"Quick, Father! That rascal has come back to insult me."

The king's soldiers rushed to her room, captured Jacques, beat him nearly to death, and flung him out of the window.

For five days and nights he lay in the ditch unconscious. Finally he awoke and groaned.

"This time it's all over," he thought. "If I go back home, my brothers will finish me off for certain."

But he was so hungry that he had no choice. Once again he trudged wearily home.

His brothers had been searching for him for days. When they saw him approach, bruised and mud-stained, a pitiful sight, they guessed what had happened. They shook their sticks in the air, warning him what to expect if he came nearer. But poor Jacques didn't care. He stumbled into the castle and his brothers gave him another beating. Then they shut him up under the stairs with a jug of water and a bone to gnaw.

"That's all you'll get from us," they said. "When you finish that, there won't be any more."

For a whole month he stayed there, growing thinner and thinner. Then one day he spoke to his second brother, the one who had the silver bugle.

"If you lend it to me," said Jacques, "I'll go and get back the belt and the purse."

His brother sneered. "Do you think I would trust my bugle to a nitwit like you? You would only let it be stolen too."

"But I have a better plan. This time I won't even go to the Princess's room, so she won't have a chance to steal the bugle. I'll wait at the city gates until the king and the Princess drive out in their royal carriage. Then I'll seize the bridle, stop the horses, and command the Princess to return the belt and the purse, or else I'll besiege the city with my army and put the whole population to the sword."

His brother grumbled but finally agreed.

And so with the bugle under his arm Jacques once more took the road to Tomboso. By next morning he was ready, standing at the gates of the city. When the royal carriage came into sight, he blew the silver bugle. *Ta-rraa!* There stood an army of ten thousand men.

"General, we await your orders."

16   Marius Barbeau and Michael Hornyansky

"Men," said Jacques, "surround the city."

The king of Tomboso was astonished to see so many soldiers, and the Princess was so frightened that she dropped the red apple she was eating. But when she saw who ran forward to hold the bridle of the horses, she smiled.

"So it's you again, Jacques! And what are you up to this time?"

"Fair Princess," said Jacques sternly, "if you do not return my belongings, I will give orders to sack the town."

"Good heavens!" cried the Princess. "This sounds serious. Of course I'll give everything back to you. I wasn't going to keep them anyway. But tell me first, brave general, where did you enlist this great army?"

"Fair lady, to raise an army like this is a very simple thing for me."

"A simple thing?" said the Princess. "Really, I can't believe that."

"Very well," said Jacques, "I'll tell you how it's done. Do you see this silver bugle? If I blow it at one end, ten thousand soldiers appear. Blow the other end, and they all vanish."

The Princess laughed. "A bugle does all that? Really, Jacques, I think you must be the prince of liars."

"You shall see," said Jacques.

He blew the bugle at the wide end. Presto! In a twinkling the field was empty. Then he blew the other end and the whole army reappeared, ready to attack the town.

"Stop, stop!" cried the Princess. "I shall give you back what you asked for. But tell me, does the bugle obey you alone?"

"Why, no," said Jacques. "It obeys whoever blows it."

She unclasped the belt from her waist and pulled out the purse. But before handing them over to him, she said:

"What a wonderful bugle! May I try blowing it, just once?"

Jacques hesitated.

The Princess gave him an enchanting smile. "Dear Jacques," she said. "*Please*."

"Can I trust you this time?" he demanded.

"I give you my word," said the Princess. "The word of Tomboso. If the bugle obeys me too, I shall return your belt and your purse."

And so poor Jacques forgot his promise and gave her the bugle. As soon as she had it she blew into the wide end. Presto! In a twinkling Jacques's army vanished. Then she blew at the other end. *Ta-rraa!* A new army appeared.

"Princess, we await your orders."

"Take this scoundrel," said the Princess, "and march over his body till he is seven times dead."

Two soldiers held Jacques down. Then the whole army marched over him until he was pounded flat into the ground.

For seven days and seven nights Jacques lay there without moving. But he must have had at least seven lives, for at last one morning he woke.

"This really is the end," he groaned. "I can never go home now."

Slowly he pulled himself out of the ground. His legs were so weak that he could hardly stand. Falling every few yards, he staggered away from Tomboso, following a little footpath that wound into the woods. He came to a marsh full of big green rushes, and there he lost the path. Several times he nearly drowned. Finally he fell exhausted in the hot sunshine at the edge of a clearing.

"Well," he thought, "I'll try to reach that apple tree. At least I'll be able to die in the shade."

Dragging himself along the ground, he got as far as the apple tree. Its branches were so laden with ripe shining fruit that they bent down within his reach. Nearby there was another tree, weighed down with plums.

"It must be an old orchard," said Jacques to himself. "I don't think I'll die just yet — not until I've had a little refreshment."

He ate one apple and a strange thing happened. His nose began to feel heavy, as if it was ready to drop off. He ate another, and his head began to bend forward with the weight. He ate a third apple, and by this time his nose had grown so long that it touched the ground.

"Thunderation!" cried Jacques. "Am I going to die with a nose like an elephant?"

He crawled on all fours to the plum tree. His nose was so heavy that he could not stand up. Rolling on his back, he kicked at the lowest branch. Plums fell all around him.

"Well," he thought, "they can't be any worse."

He ate one. It tasted sweet and juicy, and he felt better immediately. He ate another. Better still — now he could lift his head. At each mouthful he felt his nose shrinking, until by the time he had eaten three plums it was the finest nose you have ever seen.

"Let me see now. Eat apples, and your nose grows. Eat plums, and it shrinks. And I know someone who is very fond of fruit. Oho! My affairs are mending!"

Cheerfully he made his way back to the marsh where he cut down some rushes and plaited himself two baskets. The first he filled with apples, the second with plums. Then he set out towards Tomboso again.

In front of the castle he walked up and down, shouting like a pedlar:

"Apples for sale! Fresh apples!"

The Princess, who was very fond of apples, sent a servant

downstairs to buy some. When she saw how delicious the fruit looked, she didn't worry about spoiling her dinner but began eating right away. She soon felt strange. She tried to stand up and fell forward on her face. Horrified, she stood up again and began running towards her bed. This time she tripped over her nose!

Feeling very sick indeed, she took to her bed and sent for the doctor. When he arrived she hid her face in the pillows so that he wouldn't see her nose. He felt her pulse and shook his head.

"Your highness," he said, "this is an odd kind of illness. You have no sign of a fever and your pulse is normal. Let me see your tongue."

The Princess shrieked so loudly that her servants came running.

"This doctor has insulted me!"

They threw the doctor out.

Jacques, who was waiting outside, said: "Good doctor, I think I can cure her. Be kind enough to lend me your cloak and your square cap. I will pay you well."

"No need to pay me," panted the doctor. "I've had enough of Tomboso." And flinging his cloak and cap at Jacques, he ran off.

Jacques picked up his basket of plums, which he had covered with green leaves and hidden by the roadside. Wearing the doctor's cap and gown and a very serious expression, and carrying the basket on his arm, he asked to be admitted to the castle. He was led to the Princess's room.

"It's another doctor," said the maid to the Princess. "This one looks like a medicine man. He's got no little black bag, only a basket of herbs."

"Show him in."

Jacques entered. He could not see the Princess's face, for she kept it hidden among her pillows.

"Your highness," he said, "how can I find out what is wrong with you if you won't let me see your tongue?"

She raised her head to shout for the servants. But Jacques seized her shoulders and turned her face up.

"Ah," he said. "So that's it! Why, Princess, you have a monster of a nose!"

"He's insulting me!" she shouted.

"Do you want to have me thrown out," asked Jacques, "or do you want to be cured?"

The Princess stopped shrieking. "Oh — can you cure me?"

Jacques took a plum from his basket. "Eat this," he said, "and we shall see."

The Princess ate the plum. Her nose grew a few inches shorter. She began to feel better. "Oh, you are a good doctor! Let me have another one."

"Not just yet." Jacques put down the basket and touched his fingers together. "You have another disease which we must cure first."

The Princess was astonished. "Another disease? What is that?"

"A naughty habit of taking things that don't belong to you."

"Why, Doctor, who could have told you a story like that?"

"Never mind how I know," said Jacques. "It is true, is it not?"

"Well," admitted the Princess, "I do happen to have a small belt here, but it's the merest trifle, hardly worth mentioning."

"Let me have that belt. Otherwise I am afraid I can do nothing for you."

"Certainly not," said the Princess. "I refuse to part with it."

"Very well. In that case I shall leave you here — with your nose." And Jacques picked up his basket, ready to depart.

"Wait, Doctor!" cried the Princess. She unclasped the belt and gave it to him. "Here it is. Now will you cure my nose?"

Jacques clasped the belt securely around his waist. "Your highness, are you sure there isn't some other trifle that doesn't belong to you?"

"No, nothing else . . . well, only a little purse."

"Let me have that little purse, your highness."

"No. I would rather die than part with it."

"Very well," said Jacques. "If that is your decision, I shall leave you. Good day, Princess."

"Wait," said the Princess. "Here it is." And she gave him the purse. "Now will you cure my nose?"

"Not yet," said Jacques. "I think there is still one thing left."

"Oh, there is only a little bugle that I received from a certain young man. I really don't see what importance it could have."

"Nevertheless you must give it up. I must have the bugle too. Otherwise I cannot cure you completely."

The Princess burst into tears, but finally she had to give up the bugle. Then Jacques gave her plums to eat until her nose shrank. When he stopped, it was a very handsome nose, but it was exactly one foot long.

The Princess protested. "Surely you don't call this a complete cure?"

"It is more than you deserve," said Jacques. Stepping back, he took off his doctor's cap and gown and bowed to her. When she recognized him she gave a little scream.

"Yes," he said, "it is Jacques. You have treated me very badly, Princess."

She held out her arms. "Oh, Jacques, forgive me! Come, let me kiss you and make up for everything."

"No, thank you," said Jacques, picking up his basket. "I really don't care to kiss a Princess with a nose like yours. From now on, you know, they will call you the Princess with the Twelve-Inch Nose. Farewell, your highness!"

Since he was now wearing his belt again, he had only to wish himself home, and *whoosh!* — there he was. This time you may be sure that his brothers welcomed him with open arms. They praised his cleverness in recovering the belt and the purse and the bugle, and Jacques for his part resolved that he had learned his lesson. The three of them lived quite happily ever afterwards, and Jacques never went near Tomboso again.

Ko-ishin-mit Goes Fishing

George Clutesi

Cloosmit the herring, hosts in the night.
The flash of silver, the flame of your gold,
With the grey of the dawn you are gone.
Cloosmit the herring, the shoal of the sea,
Come! Dance upon the waters in a sea of spray.
Come! Feed the children of the land with your spawn.

Cloosmit the herring, hosts in the night.
The flash of silver, the flame of your gold.
Come! Make thunder upon the waters in the bay.
With your hosts make thunder in a sea of spray.
Come! Dance upon the waters with the dawn.
Come! Feed the children of the land with your spawn.

Gusty winds were here. The sun would come out bright and bold; the cloud, black with anger, would roll and push it out of sight. The rain and snow would make the sleet cold with fury, and the winds would push them all away. The sun would shine again. The Moon of many Moods was here.

It was early spring. The growing, budding season had come; the herring, in great shoals, were coming into the bay to get ready for the huge spawn. The fish would come swarming into the bay in great schools. In the morning with the break of day and the dusk of the evening the herring would come up and play upon the surface of the waters, or swish across the bay like a roll of thunder in a sea of spray.

The Indian people were busy fishing for the herring. The fishermen would stand on the bows of their canoes, and with their long, long rakes poised high in the air, they would push them slowly into the depths of the waters, cutting into the schools of herring as they raked the wiggling, silvery fish into their canoes. The good fishermen would soon fill their craft with the herring that shimmered in the early sun, and as they beached their laden craft the people would come down to the shore and take all they needed. The Indian people always loved to share their foodstuffs with their neighbours.

Ko-ishin-mit liked to watch the fishermen come in with the fresh herring still wiggling and flipping about, some even managing to leap over the side and so escape back to sea again. The sleek, colourful bodies, at one moment all silver, the next changing to the colours of Tsa-wah-youse, the rainbow. Then best of all Ko-ishin-mit loved to fill his biggest basket with the beautiful fish to take home to his little wife, Pash-hook, who would then smoke and dry the fish for summer use. Pash-hook was a dutiful wife. It was said that Pash-hook was light minded and very forgetful. This is why she was named Pash-hook, which means exactly that. Pash-hook was the daughter of Dsim-do the squirrel. She was always trying her best to please her husband Ko-ishin-mit.

One morning Ko-ishin-mit, the young Son of Raven, asked the best fisherman, the man who brought in the most herring every morning, why he used such long poles for his rake.

"Why is your rake handle extra long?" he wanted to know.

"I will tell you, Son of Raven, if you promise never to tell it to anyone else," the man whispered. "This is a secret of mine that no one knows. The longer the pole, the wider the rake I can use. The wider the rake, the more herring get caught with it. It is very easy. Take your pole, poke it down very carefully into the water until it is straight up and down beside your cha-pahts, your canoe. Then you must push it down into the depths with all your might so it will go deep where the herring lurk. Then you must peer over the side to watch for it to come swishing back to you full of fish. It's that easy. Remember the harder you push the deeper it will sink and the more fish will stick on it." The man spoke in a whisper, and very seriously asked Ko-ishin-mit never to give the secret away now that he too knew the secret as well.

"That is how I catch the most herring," the man said as he walked away.

Ko-ishin-mit sat all through this long explanation in goggle-eyed concern. He took in every word the man had told him.

The next day Ko-ishin-mit was seen making an extra-long pole and a very wide rake. "I am going for herring," he told everyone that passed by. He assured his little wife Pash-hook that she would soon have all the herring she could possibly smoke.

At last the rake was finished. It was long. It was wide. It was big. Pash-hook beamed as she watched her dear husband trim and polish the rake handle and sharpen the barbs with loving care. Pash-hook loved her husband very much and was always trying hard to please him.

It was still very dark. The moon was not there. All the fishermen were still fast asleep. Ko-ishin-mit was up and busy with his new fishing gear. He pulled his cha-pahts, little canoe, down to the water; he carried his long rake next and placed it carefully in the canoe. It was extra wide; it was too long, but Ko-ishin-mit did not care. This was his new secret, he boasted.

Ko-ishin-mit paddled around the bay; he paddled across the bay; he paddled everywhere. Every now and then he would put his little paddle down and peer into the darkness, listening, listening for the flip of the herring.

There was no herring! No fish flipped upon the surface of the waters. It was awfully dark. The moon was not there. It was still night. Ko-ishin-mit did not care. He knew the secret. He listened again. He would find fish, he was sure. He would fill his cha-pahts full of the fattest herring, he boasted to himself.

He would land his cha-pahts in front of the village with the herring spilling over the sides. Then he would call with all his might — "Ho-oooooooo come and receive your herring. Ho-ooooooo come and receive your herring." He would be a hero. He would be the best fisherman, he smiled to himself.

Ko-ishin-mit stopped at a place he knew was very deep. He carefully lifted his long, long rake. It was very heavy and his little cha-pahts wobbled and threatened to turn over. Carefully he got the long pole to stand straight up and down, as the man had said, and he poked it down deep, pushing it down with all his strength. Straight down he pushed his herring rake — down, down it went until it disappeared in the dark waters.

As the pole went out of sight Ko-ishin-mit leaned down over the side of his canoe to watch the rake come up laden with big, fat herring. He would soon have his cha-pahts full. He would soon be a hero, the best fisherman.

So intent was Ko-ishin-mit on his thought that he didn't

see the pole bounce suddenly out of the water. It came back with a mighty surge and — Wham! it smacked poor Ko-ishin-mit right on his nose. He was thrown backwards into his canoe and lay still. One instant he had been looking for the pole to come up — the next there was a sea of bright stars dancing all around his head. When he came to, that was all he remembered. Poor Ko-ishin-mit! His nose swelled and swelled and it was long and black.

The people found him lying in his canoe as it drifted in the bay. They towed him home and Pash-hook put him to bed. There was no herring; there was just a very hurt and very sick Ko-ishin-mit.

When you push a pole into the water it shoots back up like a spear. It is very dangerous. Ko-ishin-mit discovered this too late. The man had not told him this because he was always copying other people.

It is said that children should not always believe other people. Sometimes they tell things that are not true.

Raven the rook, would a herring to rake.
Down to the waters, a herring to take,
Down into the deep, he pushed his rake,
Down into the depths, to see it come back.
Up it came, smack upon his nose it came back
And it swelled and swelled to a big black nose.

The Man Whose Soul Could Travel

Peter Lum

Avovang was a wizard. For one thing he possessed a magic talisman, a dog's skin, which he had had since he was a child and which he always carried with him; when he stood upon this skin it was impossible for an enemy to touch him, or a weapon to wound him. For another thing, his soul was able to leave his body and travel separately, as though his soul and his body were different people.

It was lucky that this was so, for Avovang's wife was beautiful, and other men desired her. Even men of his own tribe, who pretended to be his friends, used to whisper to each other about the possibility of killing Avovang, so that they could share his wife among themselves. It would not be easy, they knew; but a time might come when they could surprise him.

Sometimes small parties of Eskimos would go south during the summer to buy wood, since there are no trees in the far north and wood is precious. Avovang went on one such expedition, and as it happened his companions on the trip were the very men most determined to kill him. Their opportunity came on the way home. They were walking together across an icy inlet of the sea, which was frozen solid, with Avovang slightly in the lead, when they noticed a seal's breathing-hole, one of those holes in the ice which seals keep open so that they can come up for fresh air. The men exchanged glances, and nodded, and one simply whispered, "Yes". Then suddenly, so that he had no time to use his magic, or even to touch the dog-skin talisman he carried, they pushed the wizard through the breathing-hole into the icy water.

Avovang was surprised, but not altogether displeased. "I always wanted to know what it would feel like to be a seal," he said to himself, and immediately he felt his body growing rounder and covered with soft fur; his hands became flippers, and he could feel whiskers framing his face. The water no longer felt cold, and he dived, and swam, and came up for air, thoroughly enjoying himself.

"Now that I am a seal, I shall make the most of it," he thought. "There is the whole ocean to explore!" He flipped over on his back, and paddled with his tail. But then he remembered the men above him, the men who had tried to kill him. Revenge came first.

He swam a little ahead of them, and crawled out on the ice, beyond reach of a harpoon, but clearly visible. As soon as the Eskimos saw him they gave chase, and Avovang the seal fled from them across the ice, flapping awkwardly, just fast enough so that they could follow him, but without gaining on him. He moved towards deeper water, where the ice was thinner, with the hunters in pursuit, forgetting everything in the excitement of the chase. Further and further he led them, until the ice was so thin that it would scarcely support him. Then he dived. The men could not stop themselves in time; the ice broke under them, and they fell through and were drowned.

As a seal, Avovang discovered that seals were not in the least afraid of death, or of being caught by men, for that was their nature; their souls did not cease to exist even when they had been killed and skinned and eaten. They would find another body. The seals could decide among themselves when and where and by whom they would be caught. They would know which hunters had observed the proper taboos, and which had not, and never let themselves be taken by anyone who had broken a taboo. Sometimes the great Seal-mother, the Spirit of the Sea from whose fingers they had been born, would tell them whether they should allow themselves to be caught in large numbers, because men really needed them, or not.

Learning all this, Avovang the Wizard decided that it would be interesting to try living in the bodies of other kinds of beasts, and see whose life was the best. And being already under water, he started by turning himself into a walrus. He found this awkward, for with such a heavy body, and heavy tusks, he could not swim and frolic as the seals did, and at first he could not even dive. Try as he would, his great head kept getting in the way, and he lost his balance. The other walruses made great fun of him.

"You will never be able to dive like that, with your head in the air," they told him. "You must imagine that you are diving from a great height, almost from the sky, so that your own weight will carry you down. Point your tail towards the sky, your head to the depths of the sea, and swing your whole body as you dive. Now, just watch us!"

Avovang watched the walruses as they slithered awkwardly to the edge of the ice, one by one, and dived deep into the water, and then he practised and practised until he too had mastered the art of diving. He learned to live on mussels, and small fish, and to climb out on drifting ice-floes and dive from there, but he never stopped feeling overweight and clumsy. He had soon had enough of being a walrus.

Next he became a caribou. He was glad to be back on earth again, and feel hard ground under his hoofs, but he soon discovered that the deer and caribou had too many natural enemies for his liking, chief among them wolves and men. They were always on the move, always afraid. If anything disturbed them they would gallop away at such speed that he had difficulty keeping up with them. Nor could he find enough to eat.

"What do you live on?" he asked the caribou. "And how is it that you can run so fast when you are in danger? My legs fail me."

"We eat moss and lichen," they told him. "See, there is plenty to be found here among the stones, and along the edge of the river. And as for running, why, just kick your hind legs out as hard as you can and you will find yourself leaping and bounding as fast as any of us; kick your heels high and straight, aiming for the horizon behind you, where the earth meets the sky."

Avovang did as he was told, and he was soon kicking up his heels with the best of them. He still did not care much for a diet of moss and lichen. But what bothered him most was that, being a caribou, he was just as frightened of the wolves as they were. He did not like being afraid. By the time he had seen several of his companions brought down by wolves, and others killed by the Eskimos, he decided that he had had enough of caribou life.

It was time, he decided, to try being the hunter rather than the hunted. So he became a wolf. To his shame he then found that in spite of all his running with the caribou he could not keep up with the wolf pack; he was nothing like fast enough to catch even the slowest, weakest deer, those who lagged behind the herd.

"Run," they told him. "Run. You must kick those long hind legs of yours out towards the horizon with every bound, just as the deer do, but very much faster, and keeping low to the ground. Run like the north wind, like lightning in the sky."

With practice, Avovang learned to keep well ahead in the wolf pack, to bring down his own caribou, and to enjoy fresh meat, as he had not done since he was a man. But it was not a life he enjoyed. Although they had very few enemies, the wolves were always restless, always running, always hiding here and there, always afraid. Even at night they did not rest; they prowled back and forth even in the darkness, their eyes always open.

"If I am to be always on the move, I may as well be a bird," he thought. So Avovang became a raven. Ravens were not afraid of anything. Nor did they ever lack food. He learned how to spread his wings as they did, how to hover in the wind, how to land gracefully on ice, or snow, or swamp, and for a time he was content simply to glide through the air and to feel free from earth and sea alike. After many moons had passed, however, he decided that he had had enough of wild life for the time being and that he would see what it was like to live with men again. So he became a dog.

This was the worst of all. He was neither wild nor tame. He depended for food on the scraps that men threw out to him, so that he never had a really good meal; he was kept tied up; and he was always expected to obey orders, however stupid these might be. If he broke free and wandered away, or did not pull his weight in the dog team, or did not come when his master shouted at him, he was beaten. The only consolation the dogs had, he discovered, was their strange belief that when men died and went on their way to the spirit world they had to cross a deep pit, and the only possible way to get across was to crawl along a log which was held in the teeth of two huge dogs, one at either end. These spirit dogs could hear the voices of dogs on earth, baying as they always did when a man died. If the dogs cried out, "He fed us well, he was kind to us . . . ," then they would hold the log tight and the spirit could pass over. But if they heard the voices crying, "He beat us, he kicked us, he would not share his food with us . . . ," then they would let go, and the spirit would fall into the pit, from which there was no escape.

Avovang was never quite sure whether the dogs were right about this. In any case it was not enough to persuade him to remain very long as a dog. Next he became an eagle, and later a sea-gull, a polar bear, a fox — in fact, he became almost every creature that lived wild in the northlands. He even tried being a mosquito, which amused him for a little while because the mosquito was so small and yet it attacked every animal, even man.

Finally he went back to being a seal again, which was what he had enjoyed most. It was fun lying on the ice in the summer sunshine. It was fun diving, and feeling the cool water close over him. It was even fun having hunters on his trail, for he knew that he could always escape them. If he was in real danger of being caught he had an infallible bit of magic by which to save himself; he could hide under the nail of a man's big toe.

One day, however, a hunter was so close on his trail that he was actually lifting his harpoon for the kill; Avovang was about to hide his soul in its usual place, under the nail of the man's big toe, when he saw that the man's nails were cut too short. Not even his soul, his tiny life's breath, which had no body, could hide there. So Avovang, as a seal, was killed at last, with his soul still in the seal's body.

He waited until the Eskimo had dragged the body back to his igloo and started cutting up the seal meat. Then his soul slipped out, and slipped into the body of the man's wife. The couple, who had been childless, were delighted when nine months later she gave birth to a boy.

Avovang was no less pleased. After all the beasts in whose bodies his soul had lived, there was not one which could compare with being a man. As he grew up he delighted everyone with stories of how the caribou lived, how deep the walrus could dive, how birds' feet were always cold, although otherwise they lived a pleasant life, and how, if one could not be a man, it was best to be a seal.

Knowing the nature of beasts as he did, he could also give people good advice about hunting and trapping wild animals. He told them exactly which taboos they must observe in relation to the seals, so that these would let themselves be caught. And he warned them to be kind to their dogs. They might find out one day, when it was too late, that the power of dogs was much greater than they thought.

Even the longest winter nights seemed shorter when Avovang told his stories, illustrating them with the cries of different birds, the howling of wolves, and the deep growl of the polar bear, for of course he had learned the language of each of the animals and birds he lived among. He became famous far and wide as the greatest teller of tales among the Eskimos. And although it is many years now since Avovang died there is no doubt that somewhere among the stars, in some sky-igloo, his spirit is still surrounded by crowds of other spirits, eagerly listening to the story of his soul's adventure.

How Old Paul Invented Doughnuts

Gloria Logan

Once when Paul Bunyan was loggin' on the Skeena River, he says to Sourdough Sam, the bull-cook, "Sam, I'm gettin' mighty tired of Johnnie cake and rice puddin'. I think I'll invent doughnuts."

So he just sits down by the cookhouse door and thinks for a while. He thinks for three days, twenty-six hours, and fifty-eight minutes. Then he goes inside, ties on an apron, and gets to work.

First he hauls down the smallest mixin' bowl he can find, which same is only six feet acrost, but as Paul says, "No sense makin' a big batch till I see how they turn out."

The word soon gets around that old Paul's inventin' doughnuts, and everybody comes up for a watch. "Spud" Svenson leaves the carload of potatoes he's been peelin' for hash, and Johnnie Inkslinger, the bookkeeper, puts down his pen and leans against the cookhouse door offerin' words of encouragement, which same maybe Paul don't need.

Paul orders a coupla carloads of flour, three or four bags of salt, six barrels of sugar, and a carload of eggs.

"Watcha gonna fry them in?" asks Sourdough.

"Why, bear grease, I reckon," Paul grins, and sends One-armed Ole, the Swede, down to the bearpit where he keeps a coupla dozen pet grizzlies for the men to wrestle with when they get peeved at somethin'.

Then Paul starts siftin' flour. Of course, some of the cookhouse windows was open, and some of the flour drifts away on the breeze. They say that down in Missouri, the flour darkened the sun so folks thought it was a blizzard and three men and twenty-seven horses froze to death.

Well, Paul sifts and mixes in the eggs and sugar, and pretty soon he's got a mess of dough shapin' up in the bowl. Then he sets down and looks at it. Then he looks at the cookstove and shakes his head. It takes six men workin' day and night to cut enough wood to keep the bull-cook goin', but old Paul figgers that's not enough to fry his doughnuts.

Suddenly he snaps his fingers, startin' a minor earthquake in the Aleutian Islands.

"Boys," he says, "shut the mill down. I'm goin' to need her."

Well, everythin' comes to a screechin' snarlin' halt when old Paul takes over. First he puts the little mixin' bowl on skids, and Babe, the Blue Ox, snakes it over to the mill. Then Paul grabs a coupla big planks and slams them down on some tree stumps. Makes a fair-sized mixin' board right there. Then he rigs a hoist to lift the mixin' bowl over the breadboard. Up she goes as slick as a whistle, spillin' the dough onto the board right where Paul wants her.

"Now," Paul says, "we'll roll her out."

So he motions "Spud" to grab the end of a big log that's layin' in the millyard. Paul, he grabs the other end, and soon they've got that dough rolled out just right. It's about ten inches thick and creamy by the time they's done. It looks so plum delicious that soon there's two or three good-sized brooks flowin' through the millyard, just from the boys' mouths a-waterin' so hard.

By this time One-armed Ole is back with the bear grease, and Paul tells him to dump it in one of the mill boilers. Then he tells the fireman to build up a good fire, which he does, and pretty soon that there bear grease is a-bubblin' and fryin' all over the place.

Then Paul sees he needs somethin' to cut the dough into fryin' size. He tries an old piece of boiler pipe, but it ain't quite big enough. Then he spies Johnnie Inkslinger's pen. The is the pen Johnnie invented arithmetic with, but Paul ain't fussy. He reaches out and unhooks it from the loggin' chain that Johnnie wears acrost his vest. He unscrews the top and hands the rest back to Inkslinger, who's got a mighty painful expression on his face. Paul flours the pen and starts cuttin'. The pen makes the doughnuts about three feet acrost, just a good bite-size for old Paul and his loggers. Well, Paul stands there cuttin' doughnuts and cacklin' like a pullet layin' her first egg.

Just then the sky darkens, and the boys hear the rushin' of wings. It's the doughpeckers, so everybody, includin' old Paul, heads for cover. These here doughpeckers are huge birds that live around loggin' camps. They swarm down whenever they smell raw dough, and if the bull-cook ain't careful, they'll fly away with anythin' that isn't nailed down. The boys thought Sourdough Sam had them licked with his new scheme, which was to put out a carload of sourdough every mornin' at sun-up. This brought the doughpeckers down by the hundreds. They'd eat the raw dough, it would start to rise in their bellies, and they'd stay aloft two, three days. . .too light to come down. But the last coupla days Sourdough was a mite careless, because here are the dough-peckers lightin' into Paul's doughnuts like ants at a picnic.

Well, sir, by the time the doughpeckers get filled up and take off again, everybody figgers the dough's done for, but not

How Old Paul Invented Doughnuts   39

old Paul. He walks over to the breadboard and looks at the doughnuts. And those doughpeckers have drilled every one of 'em right smack through the middle.

Old Paul grabs a shovel and scoops one into the bear grease. It hisses and bubbles and pretty soon it's all brown and crusty on the top. Then he flips her over.

When it's done, he passes it around and everyone takes a dainty nibble. Seein' as how it was so small, not more than forty inches acrost, no one gets more than a tantalizin' taste, but that's enough.

The fireman gets busy firin' the other boiler, and the whole camp works like beavers, shovellin' them doughnuts into the bear grease and flippin' them over.

So that's how old Paul invented doughnuts. The boys set up another mill, just for fryin' Paul's invention, but at last the doughpeckers got so full of holes they wouldn't come down out of the trees, so old Paul had to make a special hole-drillin' machine that he rigged up to the saw carriage.

But if it hadn't been for the doughpeckers, there wouldn't be a hole in the doughnut, and if it hadn't been for old Paul, loggers would still be eatin' Johnnie cake and rice puddin'.

Yes, sir, he was a mighty inventin' man, was old Paul.

A Daughter of Eve
L. M. Montgomery

New Moon was noted for its apples and on that first autumn of Emily's life there both the "old" and the "new" orchards bore a bumper crop. In the new were the titled and pedigreed apples; and in the old the seedlings, unknown to catalogues, that yet had a flavour wildly sweet and all their own. There was no taboo on any apple and Emily was free to eat all she wanted of each and every kind, — the only prohibition being that she must not take any to bed with her. Aunt Elizabeth, very properly, did not want her bed messed up with apple seeds; and Aunt Laura had a horror of any one eating apples in the dark lest they might eat an apple worm into the bargain. Emily, therefore, should have been able fully to satisfy her appetite for apples at home; but there is a certain odd kink in human nature by reason of which the flavour of the apples belonging to somebody else is always vastly superior to our own — as the crafty serpent of Eden very well knew. Emily, like most people, possessed this kink, and consequently thought that nowhere were there such delicious apples as those belonging to Lofty John. He was in the habit of keeping a long row of apples on one of the beams in his workshop and it was understood that she and Ilse might help themselves freely whenever they visited that charming, dusty, shaving-carpeted spot. Three varieties of Lofty John's apples were their especial favourites — the "scabby apples", that looked as if they had leprosy but were of unsurpassed deliciousness under their queerly blotched skins; the "little red apples", scarcely bigger than a crab, deep crimson all over and glossy as satin, that had such a sweet, nutty flavour; and the big green "sweet apples" that children usually thought the best of all. Emily considered that day wasted whose low descending sun had not beheld her munching one of Lofty John's big green sweets.

In the back of her mind Emily knew quite well that she should not be going to Lofty John's at all. To be sure, she had never been forbidden to go — simply because it had never occurred to her aunts that an inmate of New Moon could so forget the beloved old family feud between the houses of Murray and Sullivan belonging to two generations back. It was an inheritance that any proper Murray would live up to as a matter of course. But when Emily was off with that wild little Ishmaelite of an Ilse, traditions lost their power under the allurement of Lofty John's "reds" and "scabs".

She wandered rather lonesomely into his workshop one September evening at twilight. She had been alone since she came from school; her aunts and Cousin Jimmy had gone to Shrewsbury, promising to be back by sunset. Ilse was away also, her father, prodded thereto by Mrs. Simms, having taken her to Charlottetown to get her a winter coat. Emily liked being alone very well at first. She felt quite important over being in charge of New Moon. She ate the supper Aunt Laura had left on the cook-house dresser for her and she went into the dairy and skimmed six lovely big pans of milk. She had no business at all to do this but she had always hankered to do it and this was too good a chance to be missed. She did it beautifully and nobody ever knew — each aunt supposing the other had done it — and so she was never scolded for it. This does not point any particular moral, of course; in a proper yarn Emily should either have been found out and punished for disobedience or been driven by an uneasy conscience to confess; but I am sorry — or ought to be — to have to state that Emily's conscience never worried her about the matter at all. Still, she was doomed to suffer enough that night from an entirely different cause, to balance all her little peccadillos.

By the time the cream was skimmed and poured into the big stone crock and well stirred — Emily didn't forget *that*, either — it was after sunset and still nobody had come home. Emily didn't like the idea of going alone into the big, dusky, echoing house; so she hied her to Lofty John's shop, which she found unoccupied, though the plane halted midway on a board indicated that Lofty John had been working there quite recently and would probably return. Emily sat down on a round section of a huge log and looked around to see what she could get to eat. There was a row of "reds" and "scabs" clean across the side of the shop but no "sweet" among them; and Emily felt that what she needed just then was a "sweet" and nothing else.

Then she spied one — a huge one — the biggest "sweet" Emily had ever seen, all by itself on one of the steps of the stair leading up to the loft. She climbed up, possessed herself of it and ate it out of hand. She was gnawing happily at the core when Lofty John came in. He nodded to her with a seemingly careless glance around.

"Just been in to get my supper," he said. "The wife's away so I had to get it myself."

He fell to planing in silence. Emily sat on the stairs, counting the seeds of the big "sweet" — you told your fortunes by the seeds — listening to the Wind Woman whistling elfishly through a knot hole in the loft, and composing a "Deskripshun of Lofty John's Carpenter Shop By Lantern Light", to be written later on a letter-bill. She was lost in a mental hunt for an accurate phrase to picture the absurd elongated shadow of Lofty John's nose on the opposite wall when Lofty John whirled about, so suddenly that the shadow of his nose shot upward like a huge spear to the ceiling, and demanded in a startled voice,

"What's become av that big sweet apple that was on that stair?"

"Why — I — I et it," stammered Emily.

Lofty John dropped his plane, threw up his hands, and looked at Emily with a horrified face.

"The saints preserve us, child! Ye never et that apple — don't tell me ye've gone and et *that* apple!"

"Yes, I did," said Emily uncomfortably. "I didn't think it was any harm — I —"

"Harm! Listen to her, will you? That apple was poisoned for the rats! They've been plaguing me life out here and I had me mind made up to finish their fun. And now you've et the apple — it would kill a dozen av ye in a brace of shakes."

Lofty John saw a white face and a gingham apron flash through the workshop and out into the dark. Emily's first wild impulse was to get home at once — before she dropped dead. She tore across the field through the bush and the garden and dashed into the house. It was still silent and dark — nobody was home yet. Emily gave a bitter little shriek of despair — when they came they would find her stiff and cold, black in the face likely, everything in this dear world ended for her forever, all because she had eaten an apple which she thought she was perfectly welcome to eat. It wasn't fair — she didn't want to die.

But she must. She only hoped desperately that someone would come before she was dead. It would be so terrible to die there all alone in that great, big, empty New Moon. She dared not try to go anywhere for help. It was too dark now and she would likely drop dead on the way. To die out there — alone — in the dark — oh, that would be too dreadful. It did not occur to her that anything could be done for her; she thought if you once swallowed poison that was the end of you.

With hands shaking in panic she got a candle lighted. It wasn't quite so bad then — you *could* face things in the light. And Emily, pale, terrified, alone, was already deciding that this must be faced bravely. She must not shame the Starrs and the Murrays. She clenched her cold hands and tried to stop trembling. How long would it be before she died, she wondered. Lofty John had said the apple would kill her in a "brace of shakes". What did that mean? How long was a brace of shakes? Would it hurt her to die? She had a vague idea that poison did hurt you awfully. Oh; and just a little while ago she had been so happy! She had thought she was going to live for years and write great poems and be famous like Mrs. Hemans. She had had a fight with Ilse the night before and hadn't made it up yet — never could make it up now. And Ilse would feel so terribly. She must write her a note and forgive her. Was there time for that much? Oh, how cold her hands were! Perhaps that meant she was dying already. She had heard or read that your hands turned cold when you were dying. She wondered if her face was turning black. She grasped her candle and hurried up the stairs to the spare-room. There was a looking-glass there — the only one in the house hung low enough for her to see her reflection if she tipped the bottom of it back. Ordinarily Emily would have been frightened to death at the mere thought of going into that spare-room by dim, flickering candlelight. But the one great terror had swallowed up all lesser ones. She looked at her reflection, amid the sleek, black flow of her hair, in the upward-striking light on the dark background of the shadowy room. Oh, she was pale as the dead already. Yes, that was a dying face — there could be no doubt of it.

Something rose up in Emily and took possession of her — some inheritance from the good old stock behind her. She ceased to tremble — she accepted her fate — with bitter regret, but calmly.

"I don't want to die but since I have to I'll die as becomes a Murray," she said. She had read a similar sentence in a book and it came pat to the moment. And now she must hurry. That letter to Ilse must be written. Emily went to Aunt Elizabeth's room first, to assure herself that her right-hand top

bureau drawer was quite tidy; then she flitted up the garret stairs to her dormer corner. The great place was full of lurking, pouncing shadows that crowded about the little island of faint candlelight, but they had no terrors for Emily now.

"And to think I was feeling so bad today because my petticoat was bunchy," she thought, as she got one of her dear letter-bills — the last she would ever write on. There was no need to write to Father — she would see him soon — but Ilse must have her letter — dear, loving, jolly, hot-tempered Ilse, who, just the day before had shrieked insulting epithets after her and who would be haunted by remorse all her life for it.

"Dearest Ilse," wrote Emily, her hand shaking a little but her lips firmly set. "I am going to die. I have been poisoned by an apple Lofty John had put for rats. I will never see you again, but I am writing this to tell you I love you and you are not to feel bad because you called me a skunk and a bloodthirsty mink yesterday. I forgive you, so do not worry over it. And I am sorry I told you that you were beneath contemt because I didn't mean a word of it. I leave you all my share of the broken dishes in our playhouse and please tell Teddy good-bye for me. He will never be able to teach me how to put worms on a fish-hook now. I promised him I would learn because I did not want him to think I was a coward but I am glad I did not for I know what the worm feels like now. I do not feel sick yet but I dont know what the simptoms of poisoning are and Lofty John said there was enough to kill a dozen of me so I cant have long to live. If Aunt Elizabeth is willing you can have my necklace of Venetian beads. It is the only valuable possession I have. Don't let anybody do anything to Lofty John because he did not mean to poison me and it was all my own fault for being so greedy. Perhaps people will think he did it on purpose because I am a Protestant but I feel sure he did not and please tell him not to be hawnted by remorse. I think I feel a pain in my stomach now so I guess that the end draws ni. Fare well and remember her who died so young.

Your own devoted,

Emily."

As Emily folded up her letter-bill she heard the sound of wheels in the yard below. A moment later Elizabeth and Laura Murray were confronted in the kitchen by a tragic-faced little creature, grasping a guttering candle in one hand and a red letter-bill in the other.

"Emily, what is the matter?" cried Aunt Laura.

"I'm dying," said Emily solemnly. "I et an apple Lofty John had poisoned for rats. I have only a few minutes to live, Aunt Laura."

Laura Murray dropped down on the black bench with her hand at her heart. Elizabeth turned as pale as Emily herself.

"Emily, is this some play-acting of yours?" she demanded sternly.

"No," cried Emily, quite indignantly. "It's the truth. Do you suppose a dying person would be play-acting? And oh, Aunt Elizabeth, please will you give this letter to Ilse — and please forgive me for being naughty — though I wasn't always naughty when you thought I was — and don't let any one see me after I'm dead if I turn black — especially Rhoda Stuart."

By this time Aunt Elizabeth was herself again.

"How long ago is it since you ate that apple, Emily?"

50   L. M. Montgomery

"About an hour."

"If you'd eaten a poisoned apple an hour ago you'd be dead or sick by now —"

"Oh," cried Emily transformed in a second. A wild, sweet hope sprang up in her heart — was there a chance for her after all? Then she added despairingly, "But I felt another pain in my stomach just as I came downstairs."

"Laura," said Aunt Elizabeth, "take this child out to the cook-house and give her a good dose of mustard and water at once. It will do no harm and *may* do some good, if there's anything in this yarn of hers. I'm going down to the doctor's — he may be back — but I'll see Lofty John on the way."

Aunt Elizabeth went out — and Aunt Elizabeth went out very quickly — if it had been any one else it might have been said she ran. As for Emily — well, Aunt Laura gave her that emetic in short order and two minutes later Emily had no doubt at all that she was dying then and there — and the sooner the better. When Aunt Elizabeth returned Emily was lying on the sofa in the kitchen, as white as the pillow under her head, and as limp as a faded lily.

"Wasn't the doctor home?" cried Aunt Laura desperately.

"I don't know — there's no need of the doctor. I didn't think there was from the first. It was just one of Lofty John's jokes. He thought he'd give Emily a fright — just for fun — *his* idea of fun. March you off to bed, Miss Emily. You deserve all you've got for going over there to Lofty John's at all and I don't pity you a particle. I haven't had such a turn for years."

"I *did* have a pain in my stomach," wailed Emily, in whom fright and mustard-and-water combined had temporarily extinguished all spirit.

"Any one who eats apples from dawn to dark must expect a few pains in her stomach. You won't have any more tonight, I reckon — the mustard will remedy that. Take your candle and go."

"Well," said Emily, getting unsteadily to her feet, "I *hate* that dod-gasted Lofty John."

"Emily!" said both aunts together.

"He *deserves* it," said Emily vindictively.

"Oh, Emily — that dreadful word you used!" Aunt Laura seemed curiously upset about something.

"Why, what's the matter with dod-gasted?" said Emily, quite mystified. "Cousin Jimmy uses it often, when things vex him. He used it today — he said that dod-gasted heifer had broken out of the graveyard pasture again."

"Emily," said Aunt Elizabeth, with the air of one impaling herself on the easiest horn of a dilemma, "your Cousin Jimmy is a man — and men sometimes use expressions, in the heat of anger, that are not proper for little girls."

"But what *is* the matter with dod-gasted?" persisted Emily. "It isn't a swear word, is it? And if it isn't, why can't I use it?"

"It isn't a — a ladylike word," said Aunt Laura.

"Well, then, I won't use it any more," said Emily resignedly, "but Lofty John *is* dod-gasted."

Aunt Laura laughed so much after Emily had gone upstairs that Aunt Elizabeth told her a woman of her age should have more sense.

"Elizabeth, you *know* it was funny," protested Laura.

Emily being safely out of sight, Elizabeth permitted herself a somewhat grim smile.

"I told Lofty John a few plain truths — he'll not go telling children they're poisoned again in a hurry. I left him fairly dancing with rage."

Worn out, Emily fell asleep as soon as she was in bed; but an hour later she awakened. Aunt Elizabeth had not yet come to bed so the blind was still up and Emily saw a dear, friendly star winking down at her. Far away the sea moaned alluringly. Oh, it was nice just to be alone and to be alive. Life tasted good to her again — "tasted like more", as Cousin Jimmy said. She could have a chance to write more letter-bills, and poetry — Emily already saw a yard of verses entitled "Thoughts of One Doomed to Sudden Death" — and play with Ilse and Teddy — scour the barns with Saucy Sal, watch Aunt Laura skim cream in the dairy, and help Cousin Jimmy garden, — read books in Emily's Bower and trot along the Today Road — but *not* visit Lofty John's workshop. She determined that she would never have anything to do with Lofty John again after his diabolical cruelty. She felt so indignant with him for frightening her — after they had been such good friends, too — that she could not go to sleep until she had composed an account of her death by poison, of Lofty John being tried for her murder and condemned to death, and of his being hanged on a gibbet as lofty as himself, Emily being present at the dreadful scene, in spite of the fact that she was dead by his act. When she had finally cut him down and buried him with obloquy — the tears streaming down her face out of sympathy for Mrs. Lofty John — she forgave him. Very likely he was not dod-gasted after all.

She wrote it all down on a letter-bill in the garret the next day.

Fog Magic
Julia L. Sauer

The village of Little Valley in Nova Scotia lay on a narrow neck of land between two great arms of the sea. Like a lazy giant, North Mountain lay sprawled the full length of the peninsula until, at the very end, it sat up in a startled precipice at the sight of the open sea. Years before, a number of villages had dotted the shore on either side. Now, only a few were left and those were dwindling in size as the men despaired of making a living by fishing. At the foot of the mountain and following the line of its base ran the highway. Here the Royal Mail, the grocery truck, the butcher, and the tourist who had lost his way made his daily or weekly or chance trip down the neck to the sea and back again. But there was another road — a road less direct — filled with convenient curves — the old Post Road. This was the road the first settlers had built in the wilderness. They had come by sea, many of them, and made their little clearings near the shore. Gradually they had extended their clearings inland and in time, and with tremendous effort, they had threaded their holdings together on a narrow uncertain road through the spruce forest. With the new highway, generations later, had come new houses, away from the shore and more sheltered. Only cellar holes remained to mark the earlier homes.

This old Post Road was a joy to Greta Addington. A part of it ran through her father's land. Even though it had fallen so low as to serve as a mere lane to the pastures, there was something grand and romantic about it still. Years of spring freshets had washed away the dirt. The stones were bare that had formed its foundation. To follow it was like walking in the bed of a dry mountain stream. Greta knew every stone, every curve of it for miles, up over the high pastures and then down again toward the sea. This was the road her forefathers had traveled. Surely, she always thought, it must lead somewhere worth going. . . .

One Saturday morning Greta opened her eyes to see a gray blanket of fog filling her window space. A thick fog, and on a Saturday, too, when there was no school! . . . She hurried through her Saturday work. She thought of every little thing her mother could possibly want done — the usual Saturday errands, the washing up. Her own little room was as tidy as a ship's cabin, her Sunday gloves were washed and hung on the bars over the stove to dry. The collar was pressed on her best dress. Gertrude, Greta's mother, eyed her sharply.

"I know why you're so light on your feet this morning," she said shortly. "You're wanting to go off again."

Greta laughed. Not even her mother's crossness could spoil this day.

"I may go, mayn't I, Mother?" she coaxed. "It's only eleven o'clock, and if I take a sandwich and start now, I can be way over the high pasture before noontime. *Please*, Mother. I may even find some early berries. At least I'll take a pail."

Gertrude had been churning. She was pressing the little pats of butter with an acorn stamp. She laid the stamp down and looked at Greta without a word.

"Mother," the girl said slowly. "Please try to understand."

Gertrude's "Well?" wasn't encouraging and Greta began hesitantly.

"You — you know the way a spider web looks on foggy days. Strings and strings of the tiniest pearls, all in a lovely pattern. Well, everything else is different, too, when — when once you're inside," she finished stumblingly.

"Inside?" asked Gertrude sharply. "Inside *what*, I'd like to know?"

"Oh, just inside the fog," Greta told her. It was no use. She could never get it into words. No one else could see how the fog always seemed to her like a magic wall. You stepped through and walked until your own familiar house was gone. And then, sometime, something strange and wonderful would happen. She was sure of it.

She made her sandwich quickly, and pulled on her old coat and beret.

"Leave the bread tins and the dinner dishes for me, Mother. I'll wash them when I get back," she said as she opened the door.

"Don't be late," was her mother's answer. Then, a little more pleasantly, "I'll save a plate of chowder for your tea. You'll like as not be chilled through."

Greta gave her a loving little squeeze as she slipped out. The day had begun well, and the best part of it lay hidden ahead of her.

"Please let there be houses today on the old cellar holes," Greta kept saying to herself as she hurried along the Old Road. . . . "*Maybe* there will be!" "There *can't* be." "*Maybe* there will be." "There *can't* be." Back and forth, back and forth the two thoughts went ticking in her mind. Her heart was beginning to thump in time to them.

"I'd better stop and get my breath at the sailors' graves," she thought. It was a spot where Father often stopped for a moment. Greta had never asked him why. On clear days the village looked its prettiest from there. But Greta thought it was Father's way of paying respect to the shipwrecked sailors who had been washed ashore in the cove years and years ago. Just where the fences met at the corner of the Ezra Knoll, they had buried them. There was nothing to show who they were or where they'd come from — nothing, now, to mark the graves except Father's care that that corner of the hay field was never mowed. Greta leaned on the fence and looked down at the unmowed corner.

"I hope they didn't come from a West Indies port," she thought. "They'd hate even to be buried here if they loved steady sunshine."

When she came to the path to Little Cove, Greta drew a long breath.... The berries were thick and she stopped to pick for a while. Her pail was a good third full when she reached the other side of the open space.

The higher she climbed, the thicker the fog grew. Hurriedly, in great clouds it rolled over the top of the mountain. Then, its hurry spent, it spread out leisurely over the slopes below. Greta had to watch the ground closely to find her way. The rough foundation stones of the Old Road were the only guide. At the upper edge of the pasture the road plunged into the thick spruce woods that covered the top. The trees seemed to hold the gray curtain back. Here the road was like a narrow dim tunnel; gray blanket above, wet green side walls, no sound but the sound of fog dripping from the spruces.

It was so very quiet in the spruces that Greta found herself picking her way cautiously as if she were afraid to turn a stone or make the slightest noise. Once she stopped to listen to the stillness. It was then that she heard the sound of trotting horses! Not the slow plod of oxen that she was used to, not the whir or rattle of a car on the highway, but the sharp rhythmic beat of horses' feet. They were coming toward her! And coming the way she had come! Occasionally she could hear a grating sound as the metal rim of a wheel glanced off a stone. She stepped to the side of the road. Who could possibly be driving on the Old Road? And where had such horses come from? Surely there were none in the village or in the town thirty miles away capable of holding that steady pace up the mountain. Greta was too excited to be frightened. She could only peer down along the dim road she had come and wait. Louder and louder came the clipped "trot, trot!" Around the bend in the road below they came into sight — two smartly groomed horses and a surrey driven by a woman dressed in gorgeous plum colored silk. She was like a picture out of a book. Greta stared in amazement as the carriage came nearer. She hardly realized that the driver had noticed her when the horses were pulled up sharply and expertly swung to the right to cramp the wheels of the surrey.

"Come, come, child!" said a sharp, impatient voice. "Don't stand there dreaming in the fog. Climb in if you're going over the mountain." Greta climbed in. As she settled into the seat beside the driver, there was a billowing surge and rustle of taffeta, a flick of the whip and the horses were off.

Greta clung to the side of the surrey and stole a glance at her companion. Stiff and straight and elegant she sat, her eyes on the winding road. But at each motion of her arms as she drove there was a swish of costly silk. Greta was conscious of it above the sound of the horses. Who had talked of silk so rich and elegant that it sounded this way? She tried to remember. Oh, now she knew. It was Earl Frosst — the one the children called "The Early Frost". He had been telling old stories in the kitchen one night when she was doing her homework. His grandmother had been born on the other side of the mountain in the village of Blue Cove. It had been a rich village once and its women had dressed as few women in that part of the province had dressed. Early had said, "When Blue Cove women came over the mountain, it sounded like a three-master coming up into the wind!" Well, surely this purple taffeta would sound like the sails of a three-master. Greta let a little chuckle escape her. The woman looked down at her sharply.

"Few travel the road to Blue Cove afoot," she said. "Why are *you* going?"

"I like to walk in the fog," Greta told her.

"*Walk* in it, yes. But God help the men in boats on a day like this."

"But, but — as long as they can hear Tollerton blowing, they know where they are." Greta tried to defend the fog.

"Tollerton? Tollerton?" the woman looked puzzled.

"Yes, Tollerton — the foghorn in the Passage, I mean," Greta said.

"Well, it's time they had a foghorn in the Passage — with that treacherous current pulling between the Neck and the Islands. But you're talking nonsense, child. I never heard tell of one."

Greta caught her breath sharply and listened. They were on the side of the mountain toward the open sea and the wind was blowing out of the southwest. Tollerton should have sounded more distinctly here than at home. But *there was no sound of it*. She had passed beyond the reach of Tollerton's warning voice.

The woman was silent. Her driving took all her attention

as the road wound down from the level plateau. Greta was too excited to speak. She knew somehow with certainty that when the road swung down toward the sea she would not find the familiar empty beach. She would find instead the once prosperous village of Blue Cove.

Two giant boulders stood where the old Post Road left the plateau and began to wind down toward the sea. The road had insisted on squeezing between them when it might just as easily have gone around. Greta had often traced the scorings on their inner surfaces, the straight lines that marked the years of travel. The rocks loomed ahead in the fog. It was exciting to think of dashing between them behind these brisk horses. She gripped the side of the surrey and leaned forward. The woman beside her gave a short laugh and reached for the whip.

"Never fear, child. We'll make it," she said. "They're the sentinels that guard Blue Cove. None passes but has a right there." She paused. "But *they* pass safely," she added.

"Have *I* a right there, do you think?" Somehow the question had to be asked. The woman turned to look down squarely into the girl's face.

"You've no cause to worry. You've the look of one that was always welcome there," she said curtly. Then the horses took all her attention. The boulders were upon them, dark shadows in the mist. The horses lunged through, then settled quietly again to a steadier pace.

Greta knew what this part of the mountain was like in clear weather. To the south of the road there was still unbroken forest — scarred here and there with burned patches, but otherwise dark, mysterious, treacherous, with unexpected chasms. Along the edge of the road to the north a high protective hedge of spruce and alder had been left, cut here and there with entrances. Beyond the hedge lay a clearing that sloped gently toward the sea. And dotting this clearing were cellar holes. Smooth little depressions they were; covered with the quick-springing growth of the pasture. It looked almost as if the homes of the departed inhabitants had sunk quietly into the earth.

Greta had often played in these cellar holes. It was fun to imagine where each house had stood, where the doorways had been, where the single street had led. Sometimes the shape of the depressions gave a clue; often a flat stone marked a doorstep. Once she had dug up a tiny spoon in a cellar hole. A salt spoon it was, with a strange name engraved on the handle. Her father said it was the name of a packet that had gone down off the Islands, years and years ago. The little salt spoon was one of her most treasured possessions, kept carefully hidden under the handkerchiefs in her dresser drawer.

Suddenly the woman pulled the team to a stop. They were opposite one of the entrances to the clearing. "You'd best get out here," she said abruptly.

Greta climbed quickly over the wheel. In front of her an archway, hung with its curtain of fog, opened into the clearing. But did it lead into the familiar pasture? Or did it lead to something very different? For the first time in all her wandering in the fog she hesitated. She turned back toward the surrey for reassurance. The woman was smiling at her now, kindly, all her grimness gone.

"Go on," she said gently. "In the second house you'll find Retha Morrill. You two will pull well together."

She touched the horses with her whip. Greta watched the surrey disappear into the thicker mists below. Then, with a pounding heart, she stepped through the arch of spruces.

Her feet crunched on gravel. She was walking on a neat

path. At her right loomed a big barn. Beyond she traced the outlines of a house — small, neat, gray-shingled, — and another, and another. A smell of wood smoke was in the air. Something brushed against her ankle. She looked down. A gray cat, the largest she had ever seen, was looking at her pleasantly.

"You beauty," Greta said to her and stooped to stroke the long hair. But it was one thing to greet a guest and quite another to be touched. Without loss of dignity, without haste, the gray cat was simply beyond reach. But she was leading the way, her plume of a tail erect. Where the second neat path turned off toward a house the cat looked back to be sure that Greta was following. Suddenly a door banged. Around the side of the house and down the path a little girl came running. She stopped when she saw Greta and gathered the cat into her arms. The two girls stood looking at each other.

"I'm Retha Morrill," said the Blue Cove child slowly, "and I think that Princess must have brought you." She smiled and took Greta's hand. "I'm glad you've come. Let's — let's go in to Mother."

Greta could think of nothing to say. She could only smile back and follow. But she knew, and Retha knew, that as the woman had said, they would pull well together. At the doorway Retha dropped Princess on the wide stone before the steps.

"Please wait here," she said. "I'll find Mother."

Greta nodded. She still wasn't sure of her voice. She watched Princess curl into a graceful heap on the stone — gray stone, gray fur, gray mist, gray shingles, all softly blending and blurring before her eyes. She knew that stone well. It had strange markings on it. She had often traced them with her finger where it lay in the empty pasture beside her favorite cellar hole.

There was a brisk step inside the house and a tall woman stood in the doorway. "Come in, child, come in," she began. Then she stopped and looked long at her visitor. And Greta looked up at her. She had never seen such blue eyes in all her life before — nor such *seeing* eyes. They were eyes that would always see through and beyond — even through the close mist of the fog itself. The woman put out her hand and drew Greta inside before she spoke again. Her voice was a little unsteady but very gentle.

"You are from over the mountain," she said. "I can tell. And I'd know it even if this were the sunniest day in the year."

Greta didn't quite know what the words meant but she knew somehow in her heart that she and this strange woman would understand each other without words. In just the flash of a moment they had traveled the longest road in the world — the road that leads from eye to eye.

"I am Laura Morrill," Retha's mother continued quietly. "Retha shouldn't have left you standing outside — not such a welcome guest. Now turn toward the light and let me look at you. Humph! Yes. You *must* be an Addington. Would your name be Greta, now? Yes?" She laughed. "So I guessed it right the very first time! Well, you have the Addington look and the Addington eyes, and there's always a Greta among the Addingtons! Yes, and there's always a child among the Addingtons that loves the fog it was born to. You're that child, I take it, in your generation." Her laughing face grew sober and she gave Greta a long, steady look. Then she smiled again quickly and smoothed back Greta's hair with a quick stroke of her hand.

"It's the things you were born to that give you satisfaction in this world, Greta. Leastwise, that's what I think. And maybe the fog's one of them. Not happiness, mind! Satisfaction isn't always happiness by a long sight; then again, it isn't sorrow either. But the rocks and the spruces and the fogs of your own land are things that nourish you. You can always have them, no matter what else you find or what else you lose. Now run along and let Retha show you the village. You two must get acquainted."

"May I leave my pail here?" Greta asked her. "I picked quite a few berries for Mother, coming over."

"Of course you may," Laura Morrill told her. "But that reminds me! You must be hungry. We're through our dinner long since but I'll get you something. I dare say you left home early."

"I brought a sandwich to eat on the way," Greta told her. "Only there hasn't been time."

"Sit right down and eat it here, then. Retha, you fetch a glass of milk and I'll get you a piece of strawberry pie. Retha went berrying early this morning, too, and I made my first wild strawberry pie of the season."

After Greta had eaten she and Retha went out to explore the village. Its single street followed the curve of the shore line. There were houses on only one side, with patches of gardens behind white fences. Across the road in a narrow stretch of meadow, cows were grazing. Thick spruces hedged the meadow in at the lower side where there was a sharp drop, almost a precipice, to the shore. But the street was high enough so that Greta knew on a clear day you could look from the houses straight out to the open sea.

It was pleasant walking slowly up the street with Retha, but Greta couldn't find anything to say. To ask questions might break the spell. She might find herself back again in the empty clearing. And Retha knew that it would be impolite to question a stranger. They reached the end of the street before either spoke.

"There's our school, and there's our church," Retha said. She pointed out the little white building across the end of the street next to the neat church with its steeple.

"The shore curves in here, and there's another bay down there where you can find all sorts of things to play with. Our church is nice. Sometime maybe you'll be here on a Sunday so you can see it inside. There isn't any burying ground," she added. "It's all rock here and we can't have our own. When folks die they have to go over the mountain to be buried. Now let's go back to the Post Road and I'll show you the shore and the wharf and the fish houses and the stores. . . ."

When they reached the Post Road, Retha pointed toward the shore. "See! The fog's lifting a little. You can see the end of the wharf from here and you couldn't see anything an hour ago. Come on."

Greta stood still. She couldn't explain it even to herself, but suddenly she knew how Cinderella felt when the first stroke of midnight began to sound.

"I think there isn't time to go down today, Retha," she said. "But I'd like to go next time I come. I must go home now. It'll be late when I get over the mountain."

"Your berries! You left your pail at our house," Retha reminded her.

They ran back to the house. In the doorway Mrs. Morrill stood holding the pail.

"The fog's lifting," she said quietly and held out the pail. "I put a piece of strawberry pie on top of your berries, but I don't think it'll crush them any. And come again, child. We'd like to see you often; that is, if your mother doesn't worry. You're like a visitor from another world." Then she added as an afterthought, "Coming as you do from over the mountain."

Greta thanked her and took the pail. Retha went as far as

the Post Road with her. They said good-by hurriedly. Greta left without daring to turn back and wave.

It was almost clear when she reached home, but late. Her mother greeted her with relief. Father had finished milking and sat reading the paper. Greta's conscience hurt her. She hadn't once thought of the mail and someone else had gone to the post office. She held out the pail to her mother.

"There's a surprise in it, Mother," she said. Gertrude opened the pail.

"I *am* surprised," she said. "I never dreamed you'd find so many. It's early yet for strawberries."

Greta stood very still. Then she stepped over and looked into the pail. There were the berries she had picked. *But there was nothing else in the pail!*

Suddenly she wanted to cry, but her father was looking at her over the top of his paper. He was smiling at her just with his eyes, but he looked as if he understood.

"Fog thick at Blue Cove today?" he asked.

"Heavens, child, have you been way over there?" asked her mother.

How did Father know she had been to Blue Cove? Greta no longer wanted to cry. She could look back at Father and almost smile.

"Yes, Father," she said. "It was very thick today."

"I thought so," he answered and went back to his paper.

The Bobolink

Duncan Campbell Scott

It was the sunniest corner in Viger where old Garnaud had
built his cabin, — his cabin, for it could not be called a house.
It was only of one story, with a kitchen behind, and a
workshop in front, where Etienne Garnaud mended the shoes
of Viger. He had lived there by himself ever since he came
from St. Valérie; every one knew his story, every one liked
him. A merry heart had the old shoemaker; it made a merry
heart to see him bending his white head with its beautiful
features above his homely work, and to hear his voice in a
high cadence of good-humored song. The broad window of
his cabin was covered with a shutter, hinged at the top, which
was propped up by a stick slanted from the window-sill. In the
summer the sash was removed, and through the opening
came the even sound of the Blanche River against the bridge
piers, or the scythe-whetting from some hidden meadow.
From it there was a view of a little pool of the stream where
the perch jumped clear into the sun, and where a birch
growing on the bank threw a silver shadow-bridge from side
to side. Farther up, too, were the willows that wore the yellow
tassels in the spring, and the hollow where burr-marigolds
were brown-golden in August. On the hill slope stood a
delicate maple that reddened the moment summer had gone,

which old Etienne watched with a sigh and a shake of the head.

If the old man was a favorite with the elder people of Viger, he was a yet greater favorite with the children. No small portion of his earnings went toward the purchase of sugar candy for their consumption. On summer afternoons he would lay out a row of sweet lumps on his window-sill and pretend to be absorbed by his work, as the children, with much suppressed laughter, darted around the corner of his cabin, bearing away the spoils. He would pause every now and then to call, "Aha — Aha! Where are all my sweeties? Those mice and rats must have been after them again!" and would chuckle to himself to hear the children trying to keep back the laughter, out of sight around the corner. In the winter, when the boys and girls would come in to see him work, he always managed to drop some candy into their pockets, which they would find afterward with less surprise than the old man imagined.

But his great friend was the little blind daughter of his neighbor Moreau. "Here comes my little fairy," he would call out, as he saw her feeling her way down the road with her little cedar wand. "Here comes my little fairy, little Blanche," and he would go out to guide her across the one plank thrown over the ditch in front of his cabin. Then they would sit and chat together, this beautiful old man and the beautiful little girl. She raised her soft brown, sightless eyes to the sound of his voice, and he told her long romances, described the things that lay around them, or strove to answer her questions. This was his hardest task, and he often failed in it; her questions ran beyond his power, and left him mystified.

One spring he bought a bobolink from some boys who had trapped it; and he hung its cage in the sun outside his

cabin. There it would sing or be silent for days at a time. Little Blanche would sit outside under the shade of the shutter, leaning half into the room to hear the old man talk, but keeping half in the air to hear the bird sing.

They called him "Jack" by mutual consent, and he absorbed a great deal of their attention. Blanche had to be present at every cage cleaning. One day she said, "Uncle Garnaud, what is he like?"

"Why, dearie, he's a beauty; he's black all over, except his wings and tail, and they have white on them."

"And what are his wings like?"

"Well, now, that finishes me. I am an old fool, or I could tell you."

"Uncle Garnaud, I never even felt a bird; could I feel Jack?"

"Well, I could catch him; but you mustn't squeeze him."

Jack was caught with a sudden dart of the old man's hand; the little blind girl felt him softly, traced the shape of his outstretched wing, and put him back into the cage with a sigh.

"Tell me, Uncle Garnaud," she asked, "how did they catch him?"

"Well, you see, they put a little cage on a stump in the oat-field, and by-and-by the bird flew over and went in."

"Well, didn't he know they would not let him out if he once went in?"

"Well, you know, he hadn't any old uncle to tell him so."

"Well, but birds must have uncles, if they have fathers just like we have."

Old Etienne puckered up his eyes and put his awl through his hair. The bird ran down a whole cadence, as if he was on the wind over a wheat-field; then he stopped.

"There, Uncle Garnaud, I know he must mean something by that. What did he do all day before he was caught?"

"I don't think he did any work. He just flew about and sang all day, and picked up seeds, and sang, and tried to balance himself on the wheat-ears."

"He sang all day? Well, he doesn't do that now."

The bird seemed to recall a sunny field-corner, for his interlude was as light as thistle-down, and after a pause he made two little sounds like the ringing of bells at Titania's girdle.

"Perhaps he doesn't like to be shut up and have nobody but us," she said, after a moment.

"Well," said the old man, hesitatingly, "we might let him go."

"Yes," faltered the child, "we might let him go."

The next time little Blanche was there she said, "And he didn't do anything but that, just sing and fly?"

"No, I think not."

"Well, then, he could fly miles and miles, and never come back, if he didn't want to?"

"Why, yes; he went away every winter, so that the frost wouldn't bite him."

"Oh! Uncle Garnaud, he didn't, did he?"

"Yes, true, he did."

The little girl was silent for a while; when the old man looked at her the tears were in her eyes.

"Why, my pretty, what's the matter?"

"Oh, I was just thinking that why he didn't sing was because he only saw you and me, and the road, and our trees, when he used to have everything."

"Well," said the old man, stopping his work, "he might have everything again, you know."

"Might he?" she asked, doubtfully.

"Why, we might let him fly away."

The bird dropped a clear note or two.

"Oh, Uncle Garnaud, do let him go!"

"Why, beauty, just as you say."

The old man put off his apron and took the cage down.

"Here, little girl, you hold the cage, and we'll go where he can fly free."

Blanche carried the cage and he took her hand. They walked down to the bridge, and set the cage on the rail.

"Now, dearie, open the door," said the old man.

The little child felt for the slide and pushed it back. In a moment the bird rushed out and flew madly off.

"He's gone," she said, "Jack's gone. Where did he go, Uncle?"

"He flew right through that maple-tree, and now he's over the fields, and now he's out of sight."

"And didn't he even once look back?"

"No, never once."

They stood there together for a moment, the old man gazing after the departed bird, the little girl setting her brown, sightless eyes on the invisible distance. Then, taking the empty cage, they went back to the cabin. From that day their friendship was not untinged by regret; some delicate mist of sorrow seemed to have blurred the glass of memory. Though he could not tell why, old Etienne that evening felt anew his loneliness, as he watched a long sunset of red and gold that lingered after the footsteps of the August day, and cast a great color into his silent cabin above the Blanche.

A Child in Prison Camp
Shizuye Takashima

New Denver, British Columbia
September 1942

Our home at night

It is night. We light our two candles. There is no electricity. The frail, rationed candles burst into life and the darkness slinks away. The smell of fresh-cut trees burning, fills the room. The pine pitch cracks and pops in the fire. I sit, watch my mother. She places the rice pot on the black, heavy stove. The wet, shiny pot begins to sputter.

"Rice tastes better cooked like this," she says, smiles. Her dark eyes look even darker in this semi-light and I feel love for her.

"Why?" I ask.

"Because natural fire is best for cooking. Food tastes pure."

I stare at the now boiling rice and wonder why all people do not use such stoves and fuel.

Yuki brings wood. I help her pile it near the hot stove, for the raw wood is damp. The family who share the kitchen, the stove and the house, begin their dinner. Mrs. Kono appears quietly from her nooklike curtained bedroom, bows to my mother, washes her rice. The wood sink gurgles as the water scooped from the lake plunges quickly down the narrow pipe. Soon her rice too is cooking on the big, black stove. The bare, tiny, candle-lit room is filled with the smell of rice and Japanese food. Mrs. Kono is still young. I notice she watches

her rice pot with care as mother does. "This is very important," mother has often said.

Mrs. Kono lives with her husband and their small child, a girl of three. Kay-ko is her name. A lovely girl with black, black hair cut in straight bangs, huge round dark eyes that look very merry when she smiles. She always has rosy, rosy cheeks. Now she comes shyly to me, calls me "Big Sister" in Japanese, which sounds nice, for I have never been called this. I smile. She squats and watches as I pile the wood. The white part of the wood looks strange in this dim light.

"Would you like to help?" I ask. Half joking, she nods, begins to hand me the pieces, one by one with her tiny, round hands. Some of the pitch sticks to our hands. I look at the sticky, yellow liquid coming out of the wood. Kay-ko stares at it.

"What is it? It smells funny."

I reply, "It's pitch. Comes from the pine tree. We learnt this in school."

Yuki joins in and adds, "It's the sap of the tree. It's full of the sun's energy. This is why it cracks and pops as it burns."

Kay-ko and I both listen, and we hear the sharp snap of the pitch burning. The fresh smell of the pine reaches us. We both wrinkle our noses. Kay-ko laughs. I dab a bit of soft pitch on her nose; she does the same to me. Soon we forget all about piling the wood and end up laughing and laughing.

The table is set; the white candles create a circle of light on the wood table. I sit by the flame. I notice the far corners of the room are dark. This gives an eerie feeling. Though eyes and mind are getting used to this kind of light. On the other side of the room I can hear the Konos talking quietly. It took us several days to get used to living with them. But the Konos are so quiet, speak very little, except for Kay-ko, who talks a lot. I do not mind. I think it bothers my mother and father more. Older people seem more sensitive to other people's noises. I'm glad I'm still young, for things do not bother me, even as much as they bother Yuki.

Our first snow

We children continue to go to school. It was not the best, but school is school and I have no choice. Finally, our first sign of winter.

As I pick my way along the brushes, stumps and broken, twisted twigs and grass (a short cut from the school to our home) I see our first snow. It falls quietly, gently from the low, gray cloud. I stop, put out my hands. The star pattern of the snow looks perfect as it falls on my hand. I wonder how it can be so lovely. I touch it carefully with my other hand. But then, as if I have broken its secret, it melts, leaving a tiny, clear drop of water. I try it again. The same thing happens. I look up. Now it's beginning to snow harder. I hurry home. The tall grass and dead leaves feel wet. I'm excited and happy.

That night Yuki and I stare out of our small window. The snow has stopped. We see the lemony-yellow moon shine so nice and bright, her silver falling on the white earth. It looks beautiful. The trees outside are heavy with snow. Their dark green, spiky branches are hidden. The shimmering, winter magic light makes the neighbors' houses look suddenly beautiful. How kind snow is!

"Yuki, is your friend Rose coming?"

Yuki replies, "Yes, she should be here soon. I'm making some hot chocolate, and mother bought a cake."

I wonder if I can stay up too. I wish I were older. It seems unfair to have to go to bed so early. I finally ask, "Can I stay up for awhile? Please. Mom is out. She won't know. And dad's gone to play cards."

Yuki stares out the window. "There she is. Rose." I peek out. Then I see her walking slowly towards our house. Her tall, thin body is bent forward. The snow is all around her, all white and magic. "Okay, Shichan. You can have hot chocolate and a piece of cake. Maybe we could have it now. It's cold. Then you can go to bed before mother comes home. Alright?"

I feel so happy. I rush to the shelves to bring out the cups. Yuki goes to the door to let Rose in. The cold air comes rushing from the open door. I put out the big pot for the hot chocolate. The big, black stove is hot and warm.

I smile at Rose. She is bundled up like a hunter. "Hi! Yuki's making hot chocolate." Rose nods, too cold to speak. I laugh. We all laugh.

The small candle casts an orange glow on my book. I am reading about Marco Polo again. My mind leaves our house. I hear Yuki and Rose talking quietly, but soon their voices fade away. I feel like a princess being rescued by a brave, dark Tartar. I see the Chinese palace as my hero carries me to his emperor's magnificent summer home, all tiled and mosaic, filled with fountains in the lush gardens. I close my eyes, and dream. The Tartar comes to life, hands me splendid jewels to be placed around my hair. He takes my hand and guides me gently into the garden. I am not afraid as I reach for another world.

Christmas at home

I swing my legs to and fro. Japanese music fills our tiny room. Mrs. Kono has a small record player. From this black, leather box, with shining handles which we turn from time to time, glorious music comes. In the hot, burning oven, our

Christmas chicken is cooking. It sputters and makes funny noises. The lemon pies father baked are already on the table. He has been cooking all day. They look so nice, my favorite pies. Only father can bake such lovely, tasty pies. He must put magic into them.

Father is an excellent cook. Before he became a gardener, he worked as a chef in a big restaurant and in hotels. And now, he still cooks on holidays or when we have many guests. I love watching him cook. He never uses a measuring cup, mostly his hands. He's always tasting, making gurgling, funny noises in his throat (for Japanese are allowed to make a lot of noise when they eat; especially when they drink tea or eat soup). Father closes his slanted eyes and tastes it, then he gives me a tiny bit. He and mother always treat me special, I guess because I'm the youngest and not as strong as Yuki. She doesn't mind; she knows I love her. I watch my father cook and I listen. The old song sounds full of joy. . . .

Father ties a towel around his head. Mother hands him a bowl. He raises his arm, dances around. He is graceful as he waves his arm and bowl in time with the music. We all laugh. Mr. Kono joins him and sings. It is an old folk song. Mother claps her hands in time with the rhythm. She is looking at my slippers, the ones David sent us for Christmas. She has a little smile. I know her thoughts are with David; this is the first Christmas he is not with us. The music seems to grow louder. Little Kay-ko too joins us. We all sing. Yuki, the Konos, the whole room seems to fade. I see Japan. The snow is gone. I see the happy rice planters with their bright kimonos, their black hair tied with printed towels, the gentle wind, with lovely Mount Fuji, Fuji-san itself, in the distance. The music, our voices, go beyond our house, out into the snow, past the mountains and into space, and this special day is made more magic, and I know I shall remember it forever.

Knowing Anna

D. P. Barnhouse

They said she was from one of those Baltic countries, but no one seemed to know which one. She was quite an ordinary looking girl with heavy pigtails, the colour of new rope. In her practice tunic, she seemed no different from any of the other girls in our ballet class (except that she was thinner and had a slight limp) — until she opened her mouth. Boy, could she fracture the English language!

"Tell me what is wrong with my position," Miss Hall said one day, shortly after Anna had joined the class. She was demonstrating a common posture fault. I couldn't answer. I knew it looked wrong but I didn't know how to say it. I stood there like a lump.

"Can't anyone tell me?" Miss Hall's eyes skipped down the line-up at the barre.

Anna stepped forward with a bit of a curtsy. "Damage it gives to the eyes," she said firmly, "when body is loop-sided."

I guess I was the first one to giggle; perhaps because I was so angry at myself for not being able to answer. Laughter rippled through the room. Anna stepped back to her place at the barre. Her face turned a bright scarlet.

"That will do!" Miss Hall's voice was like a sharp rap on the knuckles. "Anna has expressed it very well. A bad line does offend the eye, and when the hip is thrust out, it makes a lop-sided line. Remember, the body must be straight, shoulders down. Make a long neck. Now we'll begin again. Thank you, Anna. Ready — and one — and two — and — "

After that day, Anna never spoke unless she had to, and then, only in monosyllables. Because we didn't understand her, we left her pretty much to herself. Maybe we resented her a bit because Miss Hall gave her so much attention. Not because she was so good. In fact her style varied from ours. I guess in Europe they are taught differently, and she had to conform to our syllabus. Miss Hall always said, "A ballet class has no room for soloists. Here, we work together as a team."

I suspect she referred particularly to Natalie, who was the prima ballerina type. She certainly looked the part. She had a long coppery mane and lovely skin and her clothes made us drool with envy. Her long legs looked gorgeous under a tutu. She was one of the few girls in the class who could afford a real one. She usually did get the solo parts too. Our class, like most, contained only a few who were really serious about dancing. Most came because their mothers thought it would give poise and grace, and because it was "the thing to do". Nat and I were two of the serious ones. She was nearly two years older but I wanted more than anything to be like her. She had more natural talent, but I tried to make up for it in hard work and enthusiasm. Sometimes when I was alone in the house, I'd play the music for *Les Sylphides* or *Swan Lake* and climb on its magic carpet. I saw myself as Odile, The Black Swan, floating lighter than any feather in the arms of my partner, whipping through those thirty-six fouette turns. (Actually, in class I'd once managed to complete three.)

For recitals, Miss Hall usually chose excerpts from the classics. Last year it was the *Nutcracker*. Nat was the Sugar Plum Fairy and I was almost chosen for one of the Merlitons. Of course I was lucky even to have been in the corps. A lot of the class were left out, which caused some bruised feelings — mostly among parents.

As recital time drew near, we wondered what we'd be doing this year and how many of us would be chosen to take part. I secretly cherished the hope that I might get to be something really important. I took to practising an extra half hour each day, hoping Miss Hall might notice the improvement in my technique.

We usually had a short period of free improvisation at the end of each class. It was the part of the lesson that I enjoyed most. One day, toward the end of term, Miss Hall wrote some specific themes on the blackboard.

You are alone in a forest. A sudden thunderstorm comes up. You lose your way.

You are at a ball. A young man gives you a flower. He asks you to dance with him.

You are a beggar in a crowded street. You are cold, hungry, friendless.

"Think of these situations for a few minutes," she said, "and choose any one that appeals to you. If suitable music comes to your mind, tell me what it is. Then go off by yourself and try to get something of the character and the situation into your movements. I'll give you ten minutes to prepare. Try not to look at each other. Work it out for yourselves. Try to feel it and it will come."

No age is too old for make believe. I hummed the waltz from *Coppelia* and tried to feel myself in a glittering ball room, fastening the flowers in my hair, smiling at a handsome stranger who danced divinely. I tried not to watch what the others were doing. . . .

The ten minutes were up. It was not so easy doing it with the rest of the class looking on. It turned out that most of us had chosen the ballroom scene. Natalie did it best though. She threw in a lot of turns and arabesques, which are her strong suit. Miss Hall made a critical comment or two when each finished. Anna was last. She was the only one to do the beggar girl. She asked for a Sibelius record. Miss Hall put it on, and Anna began to dance.

How do you know when a thing is really good? It's more instinctive than anything else. With me, it's a sort of slow, creeping, prickly feeling under the skin. Anna wasn't play acting at all as the rest of us had been doing. I think she forgot we were there and she *was* a beggar girl, cold, hungry and alone. You couldn't help but feel it. It was a long time afterward that I wondered about her limp. It must have been there, but I'd forgotten it entirely while she was dancing. When she had finished, there was a long silence. Miss Hall got a tacky old shawl from the prop box and a beat-up practice skirt.

"Anna has helped me make up my mind," she said. "I've been thinking for a long time of doing the *Little Match Girl*. It should make an effective ballet. You all know the story. I want you now to try to work as a group. You are all passers-by; street peddlars, sight-seers, shop girls, students and so on. You may pick whatever character you like." She gave Anna the shawl and skirt. "Will you repeat your exercise, just as you just did it," she directed. "The rest of you revolve around Anna and react to her in the way that seems to fit your character. I'll leave the room for another ten minutes and we'll see what comes out."

She left the room amid a shocked silence. Natalie pinched my arm. "Do you suppose she means to give *her* the solo part?"

"It looks like it," I said.

The others all looked at Nat. Her face was like a thunder cloud. I guess we all shared some of her resentment. We were so used to admiring her. She was our prima ballerina, all right, and we'd paid court to her for a long time. And now, this newcomer was trying to step into her shoes.

"If Miss Hall thinks I'm going to play second fiddle to that — that — " She struggled for the right word but couldn't grasp it. "She's got another think coming." Nat snapped and started for the dressing room. She turned at the door, and her eyes shot fire in Anna's direction. "We've got enough 'displaced persons' in this class as it is," she said, "without me becoming one of them." The door slammed after her.

Someone had the presence of mind to start the music. We tried to get something done before Miss Hall came back. We wondered what she'd think about Nat's absence. Anna went on as though nothing had happened, but I saw that her eyes were filled with tears. I could feel some echoes of Nat's resentment still, in the others. Nat was always pretty nice to everyone and full of charm — as long as she was top dog. Her nastiness just now was not enough to destroy our belief in loyalty to the *status quo* — "The divine right of queens". Who was this interloper after all? What did we know about her after three months? Not even where she lived or what foreign country she came from. She wasn't at all friendly. She made no attempt to join our dressing room "gab fests". In fact she was usually into her street clothes and away before we had our point shoes untied.

As we worked, the music began to take over. I felt the

tension go out of me. I was a mother hurrying home through the holiday crowds, comparing my own plump happy child with the forlorn little match girl; feeling sympathy, but smugness too.

A mischievous group danced toward Anna. Rose Kaufman, who was Nat's best friend, snatched away the shawl. They played a game of tug-of-war with it — trampled it underfoot. Anna reached for it — followed them pleadingly — sank down shivering. The music wailed its accompaniment of longing, of searching. Suddenly I was no longer a student in a practice studio. I was there watching a freezing girl in an unfriendly world. I picked up the shawl, shook the dirt from it angrily, wrapped it around her thin shoulders. Anna looked up at me gratefully and grasped my hands.

"Very good!" Miss Hall's voice said. I wondered how long she had been watching. "That was an excellent passage. I'll repeat the music. Try it again before you forget. This time, use your bodies more . . . dance it out."

We worked for quite a while. The ballet began to take form. If Rose's idea had stemmed from a cruel impulse, it became something else. Each one of us felt we had created something. This was much better than being taught set steps.

In the dressing room afterward, Anna was slower than usual. The others had all gone. We could hear the opening exercises for the next class beginning in the studio. Anna asked to borrow my comb. I could see she wanted to talk to someone. At last it came out, haltingly in her garbled English — an idea she had for an interchange between the matron and the match girl. Would I mind trying it out? We worked it out roughly, hampered by the jumble of benches and coat racks. It had to do with the matron's dropping her pocket book unknowingly and the match girl's retrieving of it.

The idea was good. I began to get quite excited as the scene developed.

"Why don't you come to my house after supper and we'll polish it up?" I said.

Then she explained why she had to hurry home after every lesson. There was only her father and her to care for two younger children. So that she could go to school, he repaired clocks and did odd jobs at home during the day. Every evening he studied.

"You do all the cooking, washing and mending yourself?" I asked incredulously.

"There is no person else to do it," she said simply. "My father says that the back grows to fit the burden. He is a clever one, my father. The new engineer's papers he will soon have, and then the better job — like at home. Then will be easier the money and we can have the housekeeper."

That is how I got to know Anna and a little of what she'd been through in her own occupied country and in this one; what it meant to struggle with an alien language among alien people. What struck me was that in a way, her problem had followed her here to the free country to which she looked for help, and it was partly my fault.

Knowing Anna was how I got to graduate from the corps at last. I could see why none of us could interpret the story of the *Little Match Girl* as she did — not even Nat. In a sense, Anna had lived it.

Everyone said it was the best recital Miss Hall's school had ever done and we had several requests for repeat performances.

But knowing Anna gave more than that. It gave me a lot more understanding of human nature. Most important of all — it gave me a friend.

How the Crow Boy Forms His Magic

Donald Suddaby

From the prairie with flowers as big as moons his mother took him, towards evening, into the tepee. The laughter of boys and the entertaining tones of the men faded away behind him; the sunshine was replaced by cooler light of the interior, and in that stillness and emptiness the little boy cried.

The impassive squaw paid no heed to his protest. She crouched by the embers and began pounding something in a bowl: other women appeared about her, busy as ever, silent, and the lad knew he was expected to sleep. But he would not sleep. He longed passionately for the sunny scene he had left — the active youths running in lines as directed by the big men, the plucking of bow strings, the glittering spears, the falling and joyous squeaks among the vivid flowers. The excitement was still going on: he could hear it, very distantly, and his fury against the interfering squaw redoubled in a jarring childish bellow.

"You have a warrior there," an old woman murmured to his mother, adding many more words which he could not understand, and all the squaws nodded.

"I am his ruler yet. Be quiet, papoose!"

The little one yelled even more desperately. He had often forced his mother to obey his will by screaming and it was only necessary to roar louder than ever now. His lungs filled deeply, the fists clenched above his head as he lay there on his back, and the wonder of all shouts went forth. The neat copper-coloured head turned purple with the effort. Veins stood out. His mouth became a wide red pit of din.

A change was suddenly observed by the sharp eyes, signal for quiet went all over the boy's body. His mother was standing above him, bending a thin strip of withy, and from that arose memory of burning pains on the rump and back, memories of inexpressible shame. The little one's thumb was thrust into his mouth; the wonder of all shouts was repressed, and a comic noise, like that of a wild duck feeding, took its place whilst he sobbed himself to silence. The squaw stood a moment longer, then moved away, but the boy was still determined not to sleep.

He heard women stirring the fire, heard the cooking pot begin to bubble and noticed the tent turning darker, and he must have slept, for when he looked again the men and youths were around, squatting upon the floor, some picking bones, others thumbing the last drops of gravy from their bowls. His father squatted on a most beautiful mat, hair elegantly dressed and the long chain of eagle feathers waving down his back. Very contentedly he was smoking his great pipe, the squaws watching without murmur, the lesser men offering him from time to time a quiet word.

It was thus every evening. If there was fresh buffalo meat the talk would be louder and there was much story-telling and laughter. A youth occasionally sang and the little boy especially loved that: he heard music in everything, in the rustle of trees when he had once been taken to the wood below the warrior bluff, in the eddies of the river, among the tones of men even though no one sang. When he was not very angry he tried to make his own cries into music. He always listened intently, to capture the various lilts. Perhaps best of all he knew the lilt of before-sleep — the sinking voices of the grown folk, languorous movements from the squaws where they prepared couches, his father's last feathery puffs from the pipe, the gathering peace within tepee, and the prowling murmur of the wind walking alone outside.

Late one night there was terrific excitement. An elder brother returned exhausted from the far prairies, whither he had gone to form *nahtoya*, his mystery or magic. No boy had *nahtoya* until he had sallied forth alone for many nights to beg the Great Spirit to show him the animal or bird or reptile which should be his protector through life, and it happened that this brother had been captured by the Ojibwa people and made a mock of in their village for two whole days. He wriggled free at last, escaping with but a light gash in the forehead; then he had lain famished and fainting in a bush beside the great river until in sleep the Spirit showed a white wolf sniffing along the trail he had made. Hey, a white wolf! he whispered to himself, and fumbled for his knife to give battle — but the animal merely frisked as it passed his bush, gave a playful yelp, ran, and was out of sight when he awoke.

The White Wolf, big brother would now be called. It was his task to kill a wolf, clean and cure the entire skin, and stuff it with dried grass, to be carried everywhere — even into battle — as his *magic*. And this queer object, lank, misshapen, and dangling, was more sacred than life to its owner. Every man bore with him his magic-bag. Through all his days it was clutched, usually in the spear hand, concealed about the person if the stuffed creature chanced to be small, and its loss in a fight meant deadly shame to the loser: his guardian spirit had been taken from him, his honour, his proper place in the tribe. The sole course left to him was to attack another man for his sacred bag, and such fights were always long and bitter, ending in the death of one.

The little boy, of course, did not know all this when his brother the White Wolf returned with a name, but he learned it bit by bit from the excited conversation and from the White Wolf's often told story. When he was able to toddle he brought dry grass to the shade of the lodge where his brother sat at work on the cleaned-out beast. He watched the deft hands sewing with gut, stuffing paws, carefully pickling and packing the head, taking infinite pride in a full display of the wolfish teeth.

"When this boy a man," the toddler said, "he will be a wolf, too — with teeth like that, an' pricky ears, an' a long long long long tail!"

The White Wolf laughed, "Suppose the Spirit shows you a frog or a timorous lizard, Little One?"

"Then — then I shall look the other way."

"Or a slimy grass snake? Or a mouse?"

"Hu-sh-sh!" The boy covered his open mouth with a hand, as he had seen the men do when faced with anything blasphemous or bitter or unbelievable. His bright eyes moved to one side, the lithe back bent over. "Mischief Spirit hear you."

He longed already to go out on his magic-forming and to win himself a proper name, for he was tired of the half-dozen nicknames everyone used for him, but the men of the tribe would not hear of such nonsense. He had to stroll each day to the river bend, with the other boys, to learn swimming, through the reeds, down the path where the many marks of human feet were still quite clear in the mud, then whoop! plunge! splash! into the cold green water. The men grimaced and hallooed, leaving him alone with his fright as the deep water took him under for the second time. From an eye corner, perhaps, one of the guardians might watch his struggles, frown at his baby cries for help, but jeering was widespread until he was able to get ashore without unusual gasping and din. And even when he could at length strike shoreward in the correct manner, smoothly hand over hand, no one thought it worth noticing.

On the village grass, too, where he was set to aim with a tiny bow, hour after hour, at a willow wand, not a grain of encouragement was given.

"Stupid infant! Silly papoose!" the man in charge would scold. "Still four paces short of the wand! Look how the One Horn's boy shoots. There — there — and there!"

"He is bigger than this boy."

"Do not speak back. Cowards make excuses."

Sometimes his mother walked sternly past, to fetch water, but even she would not look with any pride when he drove near to the wand with an arrow.

"Mother! Mother! Look at my shooting!. . ."

"And the meal cooking be delayed, papoose? What would the Man say if his supper were late because I dallied with a child's shooting? Off with your bother!"

Canoeing was another instruction he must undergo every third day. The flimsy vessels were pushed out, light almost as leaves; the powerful river swept them away, and in the middle of each sat a scoffing man, often doubled with laughter as the little ones yelled their fear.

"We'll drown! We'll drown!"

"Why, so you will if you don't work."

Two of the youngsters thrust a paddle into the swift current and were almost carried overboard at once, to their instructor's delight. He seized the head of each by the hair and

90   Donald Suddaby

answered their squeals with a shout of mirth.

"Not both together, empty pates! The river is fast, all things of the great earth are heavy, and men learn to cajole their way along." Neat light paddle strokes were shown. "Like this, very lightly — in — out — in — out."

When the boy could control a canoe sufficiently he explored little backwaters with another lad, or went very cautiously along a sheltered shore of the big river looking for water-fowls' nests, taking some of the eggs, which were so delicious to eat with the rough maize bread. He learned in those limpid places that flute notes soar even more blissfully over quiet water, and often he would loll for half a day toying with the small flute made from an animal's leg bone for him by the old mythkeeper, old Rain-in-the-Face, who troubled himself a great deal about the boy's absurd passion for music.

"Hey, Little Dreamer!" old Rain-in-the-Face called to him one sundown, from the opening of his tent. "What was the melody we heard coming over the marsh at mid sun-slant?"

The youngster stood impassive, shy, not answering.

"Was it 'Far off I Hear the Lover's Flute' — or 'The Dawn Steps Clear' maybe?"

"It was the song — it was the 'Song of Going to Sleep'."

"Some tune used by the Blackfoot, no doubt?"

"This boy has never heard music from the Blackfoot people."

"Belike it was your own tune, then?"

"No, Rain-in-the-Face. It is music that has always been there: the peace within tent, the slow movings, and the snuffling wind outside. Hear again!"

The slim figure, his shadow long before the setting sun, took the flute from his back and played with deliberation a sinuous flow of notes.

"It is the thing everyone hears almost every night," he said at the end of it, his grave naked body flecked here and there by crimson lights from the west, his eyes watching and uncertain.

"Yes." The mythkeeper sat for some minutes, thoughtful. "But you are the first to catch it in your flute. You will be a music maker."

"Hu-sh-sh!" The boy covered his open mouth with a protecting hand again. "Mischief Spirit hear you. This person will be a great warrior. Music makers are half women, Old One."

The Crow people were very tall, and stately in their walk, and only Rain-in-the-Face could see the full man in the slim sensitive lad before him. Never did he use the upbraiding nicknames which the rest of the village threw after the boy. He took pains to teach him all he knew, not simply the melodies and myths from old time but subtle points of counsel, the ruses of warriors in his own youth, inspiring tales, and much lore of the countryside. The very old man and the very young youth went about together — the bustling lad often providing eyes and limbs for the ancient — and the women smiled with unexpected tenderness to see them. "There they go, the twin ends of life!" was frequently murmured.

But on the night when the boy was missing from his father's lodge old Rain-in-the-Face had nothing to do with it. A brother was sent round to the mythkeeper's tent at once and brought back the worrying news that the youngster had not been seen all that day. His mother, Grey Bird, nodded with immediate understanding. The father raised a long slow speaking with everyone, but in the end he also had to come to Grey Bird's conclusion — that his son had stolen off alone, against all prudent advice, to make his *nahtoya* in the wilds.

"He is a papoose still," murmured the father, too anxious

to be able to enjoy the peace of his great pipe. "He could be eaten by the first cougar to catch his scent, and leave the cougar yet hungry."

"His age is more than a hundred moons," respectfully answered the squaw. "A hundred moons and four hands' fingers of moons, the mythkeeper reckons."

"Pooh!" The elegant warrior, long chain of eagle feathers shifting at his back, affected disdain for his son. "He is thinner than a spear shaft."

"But enduring as a slowly dried thong," defended the mother.

"Empty headed as the wind on the plain: that is why he is amused by the idle winds he blows down his flute."

The squaw bowed submissively.

"He is our off-shoot. May the Great Spirit incline favourably to him."

"Ay-a," responded everyone in the lodge, then they all fell to scratching for fleas.

Away on the open prairie the boy indeed felt a yearning for some protection from the spirits. He had marched all afternoon over the deep sweet-smelling grass, eager to get far from security of home sights and sounds, ardent to come to the distant place where the Great Spirit would truly know that he was alone and was begging for a sign. He entered weird country as the sun went down. Long companies of precisely similar hills rose beside the river line, like herds of strange green animals, each with rounded back and sides of woodland and grass. In the distance these hills suddenly became quite flat of top, square, as though a giant had slashed them with his knife. The sun had vanished into pellucid levels of gold by the time the boy had found a tree he thought might protect him in its boughs through the hours of darkness, and the western glare revealed chasms in the flat-topped hills, oddly hewn pillars of rock, and terrible jagged teeth.

He certainly thought he had come to the edge of the earth. He clutched tightly to the branch of the tree he had chosen, fearing that a night wind might spring up and blow him over into nothingness. He prayed to *Cristecoom*, the Great Spirit, saying that he was but a little man, the youngest of little men, asking for aid in this dreadful place lest *Cristecoom sah*, the Evil One, should seize him in the dark and cast him over the terrible gulf. It may be the boy wept a few tears, but Indian people would never confess to that.

The dusk gathered and became full night, black night, with the sourest withering of stars far up in the sky. The boy heard a beast nuzzling below and he held his breath for long, covering nose and mouth with a hand, knowing that any scent would be taken. The beast went away, but presently a cougar began to snarl on the hillside and there was the death scream of an antelope. . . .

For dreadful hours of night the Crow boy clung close to his breath, unthinking, unmoving, scarcely indulging breath as the ravenous things of dark went their ways below. Once he saw the luminous eyes of a skunk glaring up at him, and smelled its fetid smell, but he knew that the questing creatures rarely climb trees and his heart did not thump violently, as it had done when the unknown snuffed and the cougar snarled. The skunk sensed him so closely and for so long that he began to fear this despicable beast was the thing being shown to him by the Great Spirit.

"Oooo — oooo," the boy growled, in his very lowest register, and added a high soft squeak, guessing that an unexpected sound might drive the animal off when an attacking noise would merely settle it in its tracks.

94   Donald Suddaby

The skunk regarded him a moment longer, then blinked and vanished.

The night went on, hostile breathing, apparently endless. Big things splashed from time to time in the river, owls shrieked past his tree on killing wing, and soon he heard the distant "roaring" of a buffalo herd running over the plain, probably before wolves. He did not sleep at all. He noted the stars retreating higher in the sky, always the first sign of approaching dawn, and blissfully at length came the first sigh of the dawn wind from the east — freshening everything, bringing an extraordinary increase of movement. Birds rustled in the branches above him. Something scratched its nails on the tree bark below and pattered away. A fox gave its short sharp yelp.

The sun came up, showing again the square-topped hills, bathed in hazy light now, pink and innocent, no chasms yawning, no weird rock pillars such as the passing-light had displayed. The green "animal" hills amid which he sheltered were more delightful than ever, swooping down to river or plain in marvelous garments of grass and flower, articulated in every curve and hollow by spikes and balls of woodland. The blue sky amused itself with similar puffs and spikes of ivory cloud, and among them an eagle most majestically soared.

"A-*hee!* A-*hee!*"

Human voices impinged suddenly upon earth's silence. A party of men could be seen coming in single file down the hill of the boy's tree, and from their moderate stature and broad chests he guessed that they were Blackfoot. They were singing a march lilt, crude and limited the boy thought it was, just stumping vulgarly from one foot to the other:

A-*hee!* A-*hee!*
Come we,
Go we,
Into distance
Of the lea,
When we
Sight ye,
A-*hee!* A-*hee!*

As they drew nearer, the boy, clinging yet more desperately and silently to his branch, beheld that undoubted sign of
the Blackfoot men — the hair separated in two places on the
forehead, leaving a lock between the two to be carefully
straightened down on to the bridge of the nose and there cut
off square. They were unquestionably his tribe's enemies. The
words of their song were only remotely familiar, like a
grotesque parody of the richer Crow speech.

Without warning, swiftly, one of the warriors loosed an
arrow into the tree where the boy sheltered.

"Enemy! Enemy!" he yelled, and with the ease of a ring on
water the tree was surrounded by warriors, each taking cover
in a hollow of the grass or behind a boulder or a fallen branch.

"Down, or we all shoot!" said another voice in Crow
words.

The arrow had whizzed sickeningly past the boy's head,
leaving him apprehensive but unharmed. He bent his stiff
back, stretched his aching arms upon the bough, and
groaned. He had been spared the horror of night wind by the
edge of the earth, had been shielded from the malice of
Cristecoom sah and the savagery of cougar and wolf, only to
fall into the hands of cruel Blackfoot at the very first smile of
dawn!

96   Donald Suddaby

He descended the tree, a tall thin lank figure. He stood, not showing a trace of emotion, before his attackers.

The Blackfoot men began to laugh. They rose up from the grass and moved openly forward, shaking their broad shoulders with mirth, cackling, whooping, tears of laughter streaming from the eyes of some.

"We march out for the buffalo herd," said one, "and find — a rabbit!"

"This boy no rabbit," declared the Crow youth, with dignity. "He lies at the feet of the Great Spirit for *nahtoya*."

The men conversed seriously in their own language for a minute. He who had used Crow words seemed to be translating to his comrades, and soon they were all nodding amid laughter and repeating *nahtoya* and *skaynatsee* — "mystery" and "the dark". One leapt into the boughs of the tree, to make sure no others of the Crow tribe were hiding there, and when he came down shouting that all was well the man who had Crow words said:

"We will show you a toad, little filthy Crow. That shall be your magic."

"No! No!" shrilled the boy in anger. "I will not look. I will tear out my eyes, so that I cannot see!"

The men were laughing again. Everything of the merry dawn seemed to join with them: a green woodpecker yaffled from somewhere in the coppice, a bobolink fluttered over the grass, uttering his rippling song, a hare raced madly with bright flowers nodding at its wake. In a myriad flashes and sparkles the dew glistened.

One of the Blackfoot warriors approached and tied the boy's hands together with a thong that cut into the flesh. The long end of this thong he threw over his own shoulder, then turned unconcernedly and walked behind his companions —

the Crow boy following like a dog on a lead. For more than an hour the party walked on thus, without song or word. They were going towards buffalo pastures. In time the boy saw multitudes of the vast shaggy creatures, grazing peacefully upon the prairie, the tresses of some of the great bulls reaching down to the grass.

He guessed that the Blackfoot men were making for some ravine, along which they could creep, out of the breeze which would carry their scent, to wriggle up closely to the sensitive monsters. He had often watched a buffalo hunt and knew the routine of his own people. Indeed, he would have enjoyed the prospect if he had not been so hungry and weary: all night he had been stretched taut and wakeful in his tree, all the previous day he had fasted as became a boy out to form his magic, and now — in enemy hands — he felt exhausted to the tip of his finger nails, scarcely able to stump onward though the keen thong bit into his flesh at every retarded step. The backs of his eyes seemed to roll on gritty dust, his mouth felt swollen and full of revolting tastes, every muscle of his body protested and ached.

"Hey, Blackfoot men!" he called at last, hoarsely. "Water — give me water."

The man who was holding the thong looked round. "Soon," he said with indifference, and trudged on.

When the party drew close to the buffalo herd they entered a grassy fold in the ground, as the boy had expected. This hid sight and scent of them from the animals, and also it contained a small stream. The Blackfoot followed the course of the entrancing water for about a thousand paces, then they paused and sat down. From his belt each took a little skin pouch, filled with reddish meal. Each produced also a skin cup which he dipped into the stream, afterwards mixing a sparing quantity of the meal into the water and drinking the thin mixture. It was all the sustenance they took. The man with the thong offered his cup to the Crow boy, but the weary one shook his head, murmured "*Nahtoya*", and with a gesture asked permission to drink of the water only.

The reminder of magic-forming made the men smile once more. "Where is that toad?" the one with Crow words said, as though to a baby, but the thong holder loosened its length and the boy at last was able to reach his face into the stream.

Delicious, that crystalline flood! Ice cold, it poured down his throat, filled his mouth with comfort, poured round his ears and neck whilst he drank and drank. He felt as though he could lie absorbing water for ever, but suddenly the thong tore into his wrists and he perceived that the hunting party was again on its feet. He had to scramble up and follow.

They came at last below the buffaloes. A stunted tree was found and the boy dragged towards it for tying whilst the hunt went on, but —

"Do not tie," the boy whispered, respecting the conditions of hunting. "This person gives his honour to remain whilst you kill buffalo."

"To break honour means death," a wide-chested brave said, and glanced at the boy's hair. "The Crows grow good scalps."

"The Crow word also is good."

The Blackfoot men nodded and left him free, only the thong tied to his wrists, its end dangling into the grass. Lithe and compact as cats, they crept up the grassy bank towards their prey, bows ready, two men carrying long spears for the kill. Not a sound was given out by them upon the innocent freshness of the breathing earth. A small brown bird, filling the air with its luxurious song from a branch of the stunted tree, did not pause in a note for their presence. A skunk which was stealing quietly along just below the top of the grassy ridge, no doubt returning to lair after its night's activities, did not seem to notice them until she was quite near; then she gave a quick light leap, the black fur showing against the waving grass, the pointed face oddly variegated with white, and shot over on to the plain and ceased to be part of the scene.

Anger surged through the boy's heart at this second sight of a skunk. In common with all Indians he detested the creatures and hoped deeply that something nobler would be shown to him for his magic bag. A snarling cat! a stinking night-haunting eater of snakes and lizards, frogs, fish, and eggs! a destroyer of lovely singing-birds! — surely the Great Spirit would not mock him so? He determined to look away from every skunk he encountered.

The hunting party had vanished by now: the ponderous running of buffalo could be heard, and the boy darted up the slope to see what was happening. An enraged old bull, with arrows close to its heart, had charged at a Blackfoot warrior and he was sailing over its back towards the little piggy tail and the thin legs, wildly clutching his bow. Three other hunters were pouring shafts into the huge bleeding animal, which began to sag even as the boy watched. Others of the party had encircled a fat buffalo cow, but the rest of the herd was half a mile away, going with a tremendous roar, kicking up clods of grass behind them, horned heads down, their fawn-coloured hides gleaming in the sun.

The killing, within a few minutes of its beginning, was over. Enough meat for a week for a whole village would be obtained from the two vast animals, as well as robes from the skins, glue from the hooves, and fine decorative uses for the horns and hair. The fat of a buffalo in itself was worth the

100   Donald Suddaby

hunt. Soon half that Blackfoot village would be on the spot, the Crow boy knew, hacking, skinning, filling bowls with the blood, arguing, laughing, most bitterly quarrelling over morsels — with no doubt a rich festive dance at night about the fires.

"Hey — it was good, and quick," he said when the hunters came back to him, several already bearing long joints of red meat, wrapped in portions of the more useless skin.

"You remain," commented the man with Crow words.

"I do."

"Still longing for your toad?"

The boy hunched his shoulders and looked miserable.

"Will you eat a piece of the delicious tongue with us, when dark returns, little filthy Crow?"

The boy hunched his shoulders deeper.

"No? No mouthful of tongue from the thick gravy?"

"This boy fasts, forms his magic."

"Ha!" The Blackfoot men, good humoured after the successful kill, shot merry glances at each other. "We shall make you eat. Crow people merit no protection by *Cristecoom*. They are all children of *Cristecoom sah*."

The boy, honour satisfied by their return to him, made a swift dash to get away. He neatly tripped the warrior laughing by his side, butted his head into the belly of a man carrying buffalo meat on his powerful shoulder, swerved wide and ducked, and was up the grassy hill-side before any realized his determination.

"Ah! The little rat has teeth!"

With a quick instinctive motion the man knowing Crow words took a tomahawk from where it dangled on his belt, and threw after the boy. It came fast, fast: the youngster saw it too late, felt helpless for time to get out of its path, then received a shattering crack on his skull from the haft and fell into darkness.

Fires were burning when he recovered his wits. There was din — the stamping of a hundred feet, the rattle of chichicois, and the rumble of drums. All the men and women in the world seemed to be assembled round him to shout. He opened his eyes slowly, still craftily lying motionless, and perceived that it was night and that he was in a Blackfoot village. Over and around him were the strong laths of an open-air cage, each thrust deep into the ground and curving together to a central point where all were securely fastened. He was a prisoner, but could see all that went on in the village. Some women were lying around his cage and they smiled to observe his eyes opened at last.

The boy felt no fear, only distress at the unlucky end of his magic forming. He could but conclude that the Great Spirit was displeased with him, despised him perhaps for so much flute playing, and had given him contemptuously into the hands of enemies. If the Blackfoot men put him to the torture, of course, he knew how to endure as a good Crow should and to die in complete silence if that need arose. He thought for a moment of his majestic mother, and pictured the brief spasm of sorrow going over her face when she would hear of his death. "Look at my calmness, Mother Grey Bird!" he imagined his soul saying: "this boy has not howled, he has not winced." And, "Ugh," he pleasantly thought of her grunting in reply — "and the bedmaking be delayed? Off with you, papoose!" His father would nod contentedly, smoking at his pipe. "All sons of mine must be brave," his murmur came into the night. "How can the Crows be the greatest people on earth if even one of them lacks endurance?"

A Blackfoot woman was offering him a cup full of water,

through the sticks of his prison, and he accepted it with dignity. He suddenly felt exalted. It was his last responsibility to show these vulgar Blackfoot folk the fine quality of the Crows!

For a long time the shouting and dancing went on, ignoring him. Poles were planted all round the village grass, with a bundle of reeds bound to the top of each, soaked in oil and blazing weirdly. Most of the dancers were nearly naked. The women wore pieces of deerskin tied to their waists like little petticoats, with girdles of bright colour and of animals' hair dyed in gay hues; some wore leg-bands having rattles strung on them. The men had crests of red and yellow and black feathers, falling to streamers of hair down their backs. Their only clothing was a painted leather belt, from which dangled furry tails and thongs loaded with a hundred kinds of rattling tinkling baubles.

Everyone was in high good humour. Both men and women called to their own sex in the rough speech which the Crow boy did not properly understand. They moved in great twining interlacing lines, throwing their heads back then swooping them forward almost down to their knees. All were tattooed, and the absurd designs pricked in bright colours on breast and limb gave them a distorted appearance in the mingled darkness and the flares of light. Even though they smiled they looked grotesque and terrible.

"Come, little moulting Crow!"

The boy perceived the man who had Crow words, gorgeously decked and feathered now, removing some laths from his prison so that he might walk forth.

The dance had formed into a vast square, each dancer leaping or marking time on his or her own ground, and every face turned towards him. With a lightning glance the Crow boy noted that there was no post, to which he could be tied for torture, and he also realized that the atmosphere was mocking, almost friendly.

"Can a Crow dance?" the Blackfoot man asked. "Or do they walk always stiff, afraid to trip in their long hair?"

The boy folded his arms, scowled.

The Blackfoot enticed him by rubbing finger-ends together, making persuasive sounds with his lips, as though to a bird.

"Come out of your cage, little Crow!"

The boy inclined his head in stately manner, walked out of the prison, his arms still folded.

"Zzzzz! Yah! *Pah kaps! Pah kaps! Pohks a pote!* (Bad! Bad! Come here!)" the whole square seemed to be yelling, and there were some jeering sounds like the crow makes when approaching his tree. "Cah-caw! Cah-caw!"

The dance began again, the boy lost at its core in a whirl of gesticulating arms, of kicking legs with baubles tinkling round them, of bright feathers and fierce faces and scattered lights. He knew that he must get away, exhausted as he still was by his long night in the tree and by the crack on his skull. He longed passionately for food, for spluttering buffalo marrow in a pan, but he was on *nahtoya* yet, he remembered, and all these were but the trials he must endure.

Slowly, craftily, he made towards the edge of the dance. For a time it seemed that he could walk away as easily as that, but soon some of the warriors guessed his aim and led the prancing lines deeper around him, crying incomprehensible words and roaring their laughter. He sat down, experimentally, until a few sharp spear points pricked his skin.

"Zzzzz! Dance — dance — dance round the little scabby Crow! Cah-caw! Cah-caw!"

"Bring the toads! Bring the toads!" yelled the warrior who knew Crow words.

A large vessel, with a skin stretched over its mouth, was borne into the square, and four or five repulsive toads were released from it.

"See your magic. Behold your mystery," the warrior laughed, and everyone took up the general word, "*Nahtoya! Nahtoya!*"

The boy calmly regarded the warty amphibians. "Great Spirit does not show me these," he said. "Evil creatures — Blackfoot — bring them out."

"Ah-h! Yah! Y-zzz!" travelled shrieks of rage as his meaning passed among the dancers. "Make him *eat* a toad!"

"No," declared the presiding warrior. "He shall eat of roast buffalo tongue. Let him break his fast amongst us."

Almost blind with dreadful wrath, the boy sprang up, seized a spear from one laughing man, snatched a club from the belt of another, and struck out left and right. The dancers approved, readily believed in such courage. They pressed back in admiring silence. The boy thrust on, scratching anyone with the spear, using the club vigorously in his right hand, shouting a war cry. He reached the dance edge towards the tents, but there a stern rank of warriors opposed him.

"Back!" the user of his own language roared. "Crow! Crow! Why, he fights like two Crows!"

"Two Crows!" others among the braves took up. "The little pecking double-crow that fights!"

The boy gave no sign of having heard their words. He bent himself sharply and darted back between the legs of the irresolute dancers, swerved cleverly and almost vanished amid the crowd. A few minutes later he was at the far edge of the dance, away from the tents, and had scrambled off into the darkness.

"*Ohks kos moi nema!* (The little one runs)" he heard a hundred throats yelling behind him, but he dashed on, bent almost to the ground for concealment. Lights were lifted up and streamed over running naked shoulders in his direction. The rattles ceased, but the drums beat louder.

"Great Spirit, Kindly Spirit, help me!" the Crow boy breathed as he ran, and suddenly remembered a ruse old Rain-in-the-Face had told him.

He moved far to the right, across the oncoming line of pursuers and slightly towards them, investing the distance he had gained to outwit their reasoning and get on their flank. At one point he was almost within the flare of their torches, but he wriggled low and presently found a dip in the ground into which he could press himself. The crowd of Blackfoot was literally upon him as he got down; had he led a party of warriors, with bows, he could have slain dozens. But he remained still, still, his face thrust into the prairie grass, the spear thrown far away.

He knew that when they failed to find him the Blackfoot people would turn round to the left, over ground they had not passed, and they would not think of examining grass they had all trampled. He waited, therefore, until the last man had gone by; then he snaked cautiously towards the village again, intending to skirt it and run from the far side.

A few women were sitting by the fires as he wriggled past the high painted tepees. They were conversing eagerly and hacking at buffalo meat. All the dogs had gone off, barking, with the main chase, the din of which he could hear distantly. For a moment he gave the chase attentive ear, and he perceived that it was in the act of turning. The dogs would very quickly pick up his scent when they came within sniff of the village once more.

Ah! The boy's heart gave a bound, for it was manifest that the Great Spirit was thinking of him. Two blazing eyes were looking in his direction — the eyes of a skunk, lurking behind the tents in the hope of snatching offal, having been attracted by the plentiful smell of meat. If he could cross his trail with the fetid stink of the beast he would confound the dogs altogether and be able to get away!

With enormous care he managed to move behind the animal, whilst she was tearing a small portion of buffalo ear thrown aside by the flayers. This done, he rose to full height in the dark beyond the tents and ran.

He ran like a deer, lightly, with a slight bound. His breath came long and even, his heart leapt as he realized that he was really free. For more than an hour he forged on, until all human sounds had died, until he was utterly alone again in the hostile breathing night. But now he did not search for a tree to hide in. He found a small cave instead, cleft in the side of a hill, and he closed its mouth with stones and branches, curled himself down on the ice-cold floor, and slept.

In his sleep he dreamed of a skunk.

The sunshine was gleaming jovially on the white skins of his father's tepee when at last he found his way back there after two days of wandering. Mother Grey Bird was pounding meal just in front of the tent, and she stopped in her work the instant she beheld him and bent her head over the great bowl.

"Look at me, mother! This boy now a man. He has made his magic."

The squaw averted her head a little while longer, and when she glanced up to observe his thin frame and weary face her eyes were wet with tears.

"The Man is within," was all she said.

The boy's father, Eagle Ribs, was lashing a new war head to the most beautiful of his spears, and he bowed gravely as the tired lad knelt beside him. Brothers and some other men gathered round, and in silence the boy's story was heard. In due course he came to the account of his defiance of the Blackfoot and repeated the words the Blackfoot warriors had used: "Crow! Crow! Why, he fights like two Crows!"

"That is your name, then!" the father said, looking with authority at those who sat there. "Two-Crows! None can deny the tribute of an enemy."

"Aye," nodded old Rain-in-the-Face, who had hobbled in during the progress of the story. "A foe's compliment is the only sincere one."

"Uh-h-huh," responded everyone in the tent, and Grey Bird entered at that moment with a bowl of nourishing soup and bowed as she offered it to her son.

The youth nodded distantly. His breast burned with joy that the mother thus publicly recognized him as a man, but he only inclined his head in acknowledgment of service.

"Tomorrow," he murmured to Rain-in-the-Face, "I go out to kill the stench cat. You will show me how to cleanse her, lest the Spirit be displeased."

An eagle was soaring again in the blue, its shadow moving small and quick across the grass, and the men of the tribe saw an omen in it.

The Adventure of Billy Topsail

Norman Duncan

From the very beginning it was inevitable that Billy Topsail should have adventures. He was a fisherman's son, born at Ruddy Cove, which is a fishing harbour on the bleak northeast coast of Newfoundland; and there was nothing else for it. All Newfoundland boys have adventures; but not all Newfoundland boys survive them. And there came, in the course of the day's work and play, to Billy Topsail, many adventures. The first — the first real adventure in which Billy Topsail was abandoned to his own wit and strength — came by reason of a gust of wind and his own dog. It was not strange that a gust of wind should overturn Billy Topsail's punt; but that old Skipper should turn troublesome in the thick of the mess was an event the most unexpected. . . .

Skipper was a Newfoundland dog, born of reputable parents at Back Arm and decently bred in Ruddy Cove. He had black hair, short, straight and wiry — the curly-haired breed has failed on the Island — and broad, ample shoulders, which his forbears had transmitted to him from generations of hauling wood.

He was heavy, awkward and ugly, resembling somewhat a great draft-horse. But he pulled with a will, fended for himself, and within the knowledge of men had never stolen a fish; so he had a high place in the hearts of all the people of the Cove, and a safe one in their estimation.

"Skipper! Skipper! Here, b'y!"

The ringing call, in the voice of Billy Topsail, never failed to bring the dog from the kitchen with an eager rush, when the snow lay deep on the rocks, and all the paths of the wilderness were ready for the sled. He stood stock-still for the harness, and at the first "Hi, b'y! Gee up there!" he bounded away with a wagging tail and a glad bark. It was as if nothing pleased him so much on a frosty morning as the prospect of a hard day's work.

If the call came in summer-time when Skipper was dozing in the cool shadow of a flake — a platform of boughs for drying fish — he scrambled to his feet, took his clog* in his mouth and ran, all a-quiver for what might come, to where young Billy waited. If the clog were taken off, as it was almost sure to be, it meant sport in the water. Then Skipper would paw the ground and whine until the stick was flung out for him. But best of all he loved to dive for stones.

At the peep of many a day, too, he went out in the punt to the fishing-grounds with Billy Topsail, and there kept the lad good company all the day long. It was because he sat on the little cuddy in the bow, as if keeping a lookout ahead, that he was called Skipper.

"Sure, 'tis a clever dog, that!" was Billy's boast. "He would save life — that dog would!"

This was proved beyond doubt when little Isaiah Tommy

*When this story was published in 1898, Newfoundland required that all dogs be clogged as a precaution against their killing sheep and goats which ran wild. The clog was in the form of a billet of wood, weighing at least seven and a half pounds, and tied to the dog's neck.

Goodman toddled over the wharf-head, where he had been playing with a squid. Isaiah Tommy was four years old, and would surely have been drowned had not Skipper strolled down the wharf just at that moment.

Skipper was obedient to the instinct of all Newfoundland dogs to drag the sons of men from the water. He plunged in and caught Isaiah Tommy by the collar of his pinafore. Still following his instinct, he kept the child's head above water with powerful strokes of his fore paws while he towed him to shore. Then the outcry which Isaiah Tommy immediately set up brought his mother to complete the rescue.

For this deed Skipper was petted for a day and a half, and fed with fried caplin and salt pork, to his evident gratification. No doubt he was persuaded that he had acted worthily. However that be, he continued in merry moods, in affectionate behaviour, in honesty — although the fish were even then drying on the flakes, all exposed — and he carried his clog like a hero.

"Skipper," Billy Topsail would ejaculate, "you *do* be a clever dog!"

One day in the spring of the year, when high winds spring suddenly from the land, Billy Topsail was fishing from the punt, the *Never Give Up*, over the shallows off Molly's Head. It was "fish weather", as the Ruddy Cove men say — grey, cold and misty. The harbour entrance lay two miles to the southwest. The bluffs which marked it were hardly discernible, for the mist hung thick off the shore. Four punts and a skiff were bobbing half a mile farther out to sea, their crews fishing with hook and line over the side. Thicker weather threatened and the day was near spent.

"'Tis time to be off home, b'y," said Billy to the dog. "'Tis getting thick in the sou'west."

Skipper stretched himself and wagged his tail. He had no word to say, but Billy, who, like all fishermen in remote places, had formed the habit of talking to himself, supplied the answer.

"'Tis that, Billy, b'y," said he. "The punt's as much as one hand can manage in a fair wind. An' 'tis a dead beat to the harbour now."

Then Billy said a word for himself. "We'll put in for ballast. The punt's too light for a gale."

He sculled the punt to the little cove by the Head, and there loaded her with rocks. Her sails, mainsail and tiny jib, were spread, and she was pointed for Grassy Island, on the first leg of her beat into the wind. By this time two other punts were under way, and the sails of the skiff were fluttering as her crew prepared to beat home for the night. The *Never Give Up* was ahead of the fleet, and held her lead in such fine fashion as made Billy Topsail's heart swell with pride.

The wind had gained in force. It was sweeping down from the hills in gusts. Now it fell to a breeze, and again it came swiftly with angry strength. Nor could its advance be perceived, for the sea was choppy and the bluffs shielded the inshore waters.

"We'll fetch the harbour on the next tack," Billy muttered to Skipper, who was whining in the bow.

He put the steering oar hard alee to bring the punt about. A gust caught the sails. The boat heeled before it, and her gunwale was under water before Billy could make a move to save her. The wind forced her down, pressing heavily upon the canvas.

"Easy!" screamed Billy.

But the ballast of the *Never Give Up* shifted, and she toppled over. Boy and dog were thrown into the sea — the one

aft, the other forward. Billy dived deep to escape entanglement with the rigging of the boat. He had long ago learned the lesson that presence of mind wins half the fight in perilous emergencies. The coward miserably perishes where the brave man survives. With his courage leaping to meet his predicament, he struck out for windward and rose to the surface.

He looked about for the punt. She had been heavily weighted with ballast, and he feared for her. What was he to do if she had been too heavily weighted? Even as he looked she sank. She had righted under water; the tip of the mast was the last he saw of her.

The sea — cold, fretful, vast — lay all about him. The coast was half a mile to windward; the punts, out to sea, were laboriously beating towards him, and could make no greater speed. He had to choose between the punts and the rocks.

A whine — with a strange note in it — attracted his attention. The big dog had caught sight of him, and was beating the water in a frantic effort to approach quickly. But the dog had never whined like that before.

"Hi, Skipper!" Billy called. "Steady, b'y! Steady!"

Billy took off his boots as fast as he could. The dog was coming nearer, still whining strangely, and madly pawing the water. Billy was mystified. What possessed the dog? It was as if he had been seized with a fit of terror. Was he afraid of drowning? His eyes were fairly flaring. Such a light had never been in them before.

In the instant he had for speculation the boy lifted himself high in the water and looked intently into the dog's eyes. It was terror he saw in them; there could be no doubt about that, he thought. The dog was afraid for his life. At once Billy was filled with dread. He could not crush the feeling down. Afraid of Skipper — the old, affectionate Skipper — his own dog, which he had reared from a puppy! It was absurd.

But he *was* afraid, nevertheless — and he was desperately afraid.

"Back, b'y!" he cried. "Get back, sir!"

It chanced that Billy Topsail was a strong swimmer. He had learned to swim where the water is cold — cold, often, as the icebergs stranded in the harbour can make it. The water was bitter cold now; but he did not fear it; nor did he doubt that he could accomplish the long swim which lay before him. It was the unaccountable behaviour of the dog which disturbed him — his failure in obedience, which could not be explained. The dog was now within three yards, and excited past all reason.

"Back, sir!" Billy screamed. "Get back with you!"

Skipper was not deterred by the command. He did not so much as hesitate. Billy raised his hand as if to strike him — a threatening gesture which had sent Skipper home with his tail between his legs many a time. But it had no effect now.

"Get back!" Billy screamed again.

It was plain that the dog was not to be bidden. Billy threw himself on his back, supported himself with his hands and kicked at the dog with his feet.

Skipper was blinded by the splashing. He whined and held back. Then blindly he came again. Billy moved slowly from him, head foremost, still churning the water with his feet. But, swimming thus, he was no match for the dog. With his head thrown back to escape the blows, Skipper forged after him. He was struck in the jaws, in the throat and again in the jaws. But he pawed on, taking every blow without complaint, and gaining inch by inch. Soon he was so close that the lad could no longer move his feet freely. Then the dog chanced to catch one foot with his paw, and forced it under. Billy could not beat him off.

No longer opposed, the dog crept up — paw over paw, forcing the boy's body lower and lower. His object was clear to Billy. Skipper, frenzied by terror, the boy thought, would try to save himself by climbing on his shoulders.

"Skipper!" he cried. "You'll drown me! Get back!"

The futility of attempting to command obedience from a crazy dog struck Billy Topsail with force. He must act otherwise, and that quickly, if he were to escape. There seemed to be but one thing to do. He took a long breath and let himself sink — down — down — as deep as he dared. Down — down — until he retained breath sufficient but to strike to the right and rise again.

The dog — as it was made known later — rose as high as he could force himself, and looked about in every direction, with his mouth open and his ears rigidly cocked. He gave two sharp barks, like sobs, and a long, mournful whine. Then, as if acting upon sudden thought, he dived.

For a moment nothing was to be seen of either boy or dog. There was nothing but a choppy sea in that place. Men who were watching thought that both had followed the *Never Give Up* to the bottom.

In the momentary respite under water Billy perceived that his situation was desperate. He would rise, he was sure, but only to renew the struggle. How long he could keep the dog off he could not tell. Until the punts came down to his aid? He thought not.

He came to the surface prepared to dive again. But Skipper had disappeared. An ejaculation of thanksgiving was yet on the boy's lips when the dog's black head rose and moved swiftly towards him. Billy had a start of ten yards — or something more.

He turned on his side and set off at top speed. There was no better swimmer among the lads of the harbour. Was he a match for a powerful Newfoundland dog? It was soon evident that he was not.

Skipper gained rapidly. Billy felt a paw strike his foot. He put more strength into his strokes. Next the paw struck the calf of his leg. The dog was upon him now — pawing his back. Billy could not sustain the weight. To escape, that he might take up the fight in another way, he dived again.

The dog was waiting when Billy came up — waiting eagerly, on the alert to continue the chase.

"Skipper, old fellow — good old dog!" Billy called in a soothing voice. "Steady, sir! Down, sir — back!"

The dog was not to be deceived. He came, by turns whining and gasping. He was more excited, more determined, than ever. Billy waited for him. The fight was to be face to face. The boy had determined to keep him off with his hands until strength failed — to drown him if he could. All love for the dog had gone out of his heart. The weeks of close and merry companionship, of romps and rambles and sport, were forgotten. Billy was fighting for life. So he waited without pity, hoping only that his strength might last until he had conquered.

When the dog was within reach Billy struck him in the face. A snarl and an angry snap were the result.

Rage seemed suddenly to possess the dog. He held back for a moment, growling fiercely, and then attacked with a rush. Billy fought as best he could, trying to clutch his enemy by the neck and to force his head beneath the waves. The effort was vain; the dog eluded his grasp and renewed the attack. In another moment he had laid his heavy paws on the boy's shoulders.

The weight was too much for Billy. Down he went; freed

116 Norman Duncan

himself, and struggled to the surface, gasping for breath. It appeared to him now that he had but a moment to live. He felt his self-possession going from him — and at that moment his ears caught the sound of a voice.

"Put your arm — "

The voice seemed to come from far away. Before the sentence was completed, the dog's paws were again on Billy's shoulders and the water stopped the boy's hearing. What were they calling to him? The thought that some helping hand was near inspired him. With this new courage to aid, he dived for the third time. The voice was nearer — clearer — when he came up, and he heard every word.

"Put your arm around his neck!" one man cried.

"Catch him by the scruff of the neck!" cried another.

Billy's self-possession returned. He would follow this direction. Skipper swam anxiously to him. It may be that he wondered what this new attitude meant. It may be that he hoped reason had returned to the boy — that at last he would allow himself to be saved. Billy caught the dog by the scruff of the neck when he was within arm's length. Skipper wagged his tail and turned about.

There was a brief pause, during which the faithful old dog determined upon the direction he would take. He espied the punts, which had borne down with all speed. Towards them he swam, and there was something of pride in his mighty strokes, something of exultation in his whine. Billy struck out with his free hand, and soon boy and dog were pulled over the side of the nearest punt.

Through it all, as Billy now knew, the dog had only wanted to save him.

That night Billy Topsail took Skipper aside for a long and confidential talk. "Skipper," said he, "I beg your pardon. You see, I didn't know what 'twas you wanted. I'm sorry I ever had a hard thought against you, and I'm sorry I tried to drown you. When I thought you only wanted to save yourself, 'twas Billy Topsail you were thinking of. When I thought you wanted to climb atop of me, 'twas my collar you wanted to catch. When I thought you wanted to bite me, 'twas a scolding you were giving me for my foolishness. Skipper, b'y, honest, I beg your pardon. Next time I'll know that all a Newfoundland dog wants is half a chance to tow me ashore. And I'll give him a whole chance. But, Skipper, don't you think you might have given me a chance to do something for myself?"

At which Skipper wagged his tail.

Little Baptiste

E. W. Thomson

Ma'ame Baptiste Larocque peered again into her cupboard and her flour barrel, as though she might have been mistaken in her inspection twenty minutes earlier.

"No, there is nothing, nothing at all!" said she to her old mother-in-law. "And no more trust at the store. Monsieur Conolly was too cross when I went for corn-meal yesterday. For sure, Baptiste stays very long at the shanty this year."

"Fear nothing, Delima," answered the bright-eyed old woman. "The good God will send a breakfast for the little ones, and for us. In seventy years I do not know Him to fail once, my daughter. Baptiste may be back tomorrow, and with more money for staying so long. No, no; fear not, Delima! *Le bon Dieu* manages all for the best."

"That is true; for so I have heard always," answered Delima, with conviction; "but sometimes *le bon Dieu* requires one's inside to pray very loud. Certainly I trust, like you, *Memere*; but it would be pleasant if He would send the food the day before."

"Ah, you are too anxious, like little Baptiste here," and the old woman glanced at the boy sitting by the cradle. "Young folks did not talk so when I was little. Then we did not think there was danger in trusting *Monsieur le Curé* when he told us to take no heed of the morrow. But now! to hear them talk, one might think they had never heard of *le bon Dieu*. The young people think too much, for sure. Trust in the good God, I say. Breakfast and dinner and supper too we shall all have tomorrow."

"Yes, *Memere*," replied the boy, who was called little Baptiste to distinguish him from his father. "*Le bon Dieu* will send an excellent breakfast, sure enough. If I get up very early, and find some good *doré* (pickerel) and catfish on the night-line. But if I did not bait the hooks, what then? Well, I hope there will be more tomorrow than this morning, anyway."

"There were enough," said the old woman, severely. "Have we not had plenty all day, Delima?"

Delima made no answer. She was in doubt about the plenty which her mother-in-law spoke of. She wondered whether small André and Odillon and 'Toinette, whose heavy breathing she could hear through the thin partition, would have been sleeping so peacefully had little Baptiste not divided his share among them at supper-time, with the excuse that he did not feel very well?

Delima was young yet, — though little Baptiste was such a big boy, — and would have rested fully on the positively expressed trust of her mother-in-law, in spite of the empty flour barrel, if she had not suspected little Baptiste of sitting there hungry.

However, he was such a strange boy, she soon reflected, that perhaps going empty did not make him feel bad! Little Baptiste was so decided in his ways, made what in others would have been sacrifices so much as a matter of course, and was so much disgusted on being offered credit or sympathy in consequence, that his mother, not being able to understand him, was not a little afraid of him.

He was not very formidable in appearance, however, that clumsy boy of fourteen or so, whose big freckled, good face was now bent over the cradle where *la petite* Seraphine lay smiling in her sleep, with soft little fingers clutched round his rough one.

"For sure," said Delima, observing the baby's smile, "the good angels are very near. I wonder what they are telling her?"

"Something about her father, of course; for so I have always heard it is when the infants smile in sleep," answered the old woman.

Little Baptiste rose impatiently and went into the sleeping-room. Often the simplicity and sentimentality of his mother and grandmother gave him strange pangs at heart; they seemed to be the children, while he felt very old. They were always looking for wonderful things to happen, and expecting the saints and *le bon Dieu* to help the family out of difficulties that little Baptiste saw no way of overcoming without the work which was then so hard to get. His mother's remark about the angels talking to little Seraphine pained him so much that he would have cried had he not felt compelled to be very much of a man during his father's absence.

If he had been asked to name the spirit hovering about, he would have mentioned a very wicked one as personified in John Conolly, the village storekeeper, the vampire of the little hamlet a quarter of a mile distant. Conolly owned the tavern too, and a sawmill upriver, and altogether was a very rich, powerful, and dreadful person in little Baptiste's view. Worst of all, he practically owned the cabin and lot of the Larocques, for he had made big Baptiste give him a bill of sale of the place as security for groceries to be advanced to the family while its head was away in the shanty; and that afternoon Conolly had said to little Baptiste that the credit had been exhausted, and more.

"No; you can't get any pork," said the storekeeper. "Don't your mother know that, after me sending her away when she wanted corn-meal yesterday? Tell her she don't get another cent's worth here."

"For why not? My fader always he pay," said the indignant boy, trying to talk English.

"Yes, indeed! Well, he ain't paid this time. How do I know what's happened to him, as he ain't back from the shanty? Tell you what: I'm going to turn you all out if your mother don't pay rent in advance for the shanty tomorrow, — four dollars a month."

"What you talkin' so for? We doan' goin' pay no rent for our own house!"

"You doan' goin' to own no house," answered Conolly, mimicking the boy. "The house is mine any time I like to say so. If the store bill ain't paid tonight, out you go tomorrow, or else pay rent. Tell your mother that for me. Mosey off now. '*Marche, donc!*' There's no other way."

Little Baptiste had not told his mother of this terrible threat, for what was the use? She had no money. He knew that she would begin weeping and wailing, with small André and Odillon as a puzzled, excited chorus, with 'Toinette and Seraphine adding those baby cries that made little Baptiste want to cry himself; with his grandmother steadily advising, in the din, that patient trust in *le bon Dieu* which he could not always entertain, though he felt very wretched that he could not.

Moreover, he desired to spare his mother and grandmother as long as possible. "Let them have their good night's sleep," said he to himself, with such thoughtfulness and pity as a merchant might feel in concealing imminent bankruptcy from his family. He knew there was but one chance remaining, — that his father might come home during the night or next morning, with his winter's wages.

Big Baptiste had "gone up" for Rewbell the jobber; had gone in November, to make logs in the distant Petawawa woods, and now the month was May. The "very magnificent" pig he had salted down before going away had been eaten long ago. My! what a time it seemed now to little Baptiste since that pig-killing! How good the *boudin* (the blood-puddings) had been, and the liver and tender bits, and what a joyful time they had had! The barrelful of salted pike and catfish was all gone too, — which made the fact that the fish were not biting well this year very sad indeed.

Now on top of all these troubles this new danger of being turned out on the roadside! For where are they to get four dollars, or two, or one even, to stave Conolly off? Certainly his father was away too long; but surely, surely, thought the boy, he would get back in time to save his home! Then he remembered with horror, and a feeling of being disloyal to his father for remembering, that terrible day, three years before, when big Baptiste had come back from his winter's work drunk, and without a dollar, having been robbed while on a spree in Ottawa. If that were the reason of his father's delay now, ah, then there would be no hope, unless *le bon Dieu* should indeed work a miracle for them!

While the boy thought over the situation with fear, his grandmother went to her bed, and soon afterward Delima took the little Seraphine's cradle into the sleeping-room. That left little Baptiste so lonely that he could not sit still: nor did he see any use of going to lie awake in bed by André and Odillon.

So he left the cabin softly, and reaching the river with a few steps, pushed off his flat-bottomed boat, and was carried smartly upstream by the shore eddy. It soon gave him to the current, and then he drifted idly down under the bright moon, listening to the roar of the long rapid, near the foot of which their cabin stood. Then he took to his oars, and rowed to the end of his night-line, tied to the wharf. He had an unusual fear that it might be gone, but found it all right, stretched taut; a slender rope, four hundred feet long, floated here and there far away in the darkness by flat cedar sticks, — a rope carrying short bits of line, and forty hooks, all loaded with excellent fat, wriggling worms.

That day little Baptiste had taken much trouble with his night-line; he was proud of the plentiful bait, and now, as he felt the tightened rope with his fingers, he told himself that his well-filled hooks *must* attract plenty of fish, — perhaps a sturgeon! Wouldn't that be grand? A big sturgeon of seventy-five pounds!

He pondered the Ottawa statement that "there are seven kinds of meat on the head of a sturgeon," and, enumerating the kinds, fell into a conviction that one sturgeon at least would surely come to his line. Had not three been caught in one night by Pierre Mallette, who had no sort of claim, who was too lazy to bait more than half his hooks, altogether too wicked to receive any special favors from *le bon Dieu*?

Little Baptiste rowed home, entered the cabin softly, and stripped for bed, almost happy in guessing what the big fish would probably weigh.

Putting his arms around little André, he tried to go to sleep; but the threats of Conolly came to him with new force, and he lay awake, with a heavy dread in his heart.

How long he had been lying thus he did not know, when a

heavy step came upon the plank outside the door.

"Father's home!" cried little Baptiste, springing to the floor as the door opened.

"Baptiste! my own Baptiste!" cried Delima, putting her arms around her husband as he stood over her.

"Did I not say," said the old woman, seizing her son's hand, "that the good God would send help in time?"

Little Baptiste lit the lamp. Then they saw something in the father's face that startled them all. He had not spoken, and now they perceived that he was haggard, pale, wild-eyed.

"The good God!" cried big Baptiste, and knelt by the bed, and bowed his head on his arms, and wept so loudly that little André and Odillon, wakening, joined his cry. "*Le bon Dieu* has forgotten us! For all my winter's work I have not one dollar! The concern is failed. Rewbell paid not one cent of wages, but ran away, and the timber has been seized."

Oh, the heartbreak! Oh, poor Delima! poor children! and poor little Baptiste, with the threats of Conolly rending his heart!

"I have walked all day," said his father, "and eaten not a thing. Give me something, Delima."

"O holy angels!" cried the poor woman, breaking into a wild weeping. "O Baptiste, Baptiste, my poor man! There is nothing; not a scrap; not any flour, not meal, not grease even; not a pinch of tea!" but still she searched frantically about the rooms.

"Never mind," said big Baptiste then, holding her in his strong arms. "I am not so hungry as tired, Delima, and I can sleep."

The old woman, who had been swaying to and fro in her chair of rushes, rose now, and laid her aged hands on the broad shoulders of the man.

"My son Baptiste," she said, "you must not say that God has forgotten us, for He has not forgotten us. The hunger is hard to bear, I know, — hard, hard to bear; but great plenty will be sent in answer to our prayers. And it is hard, hard to lose thy long winter's work; but be patient, my son, and thankful, yes, thankful for all thou hast.

"Behold, Delima is well and strong. See the little Baptiste, how much a man! Yes, that is right; kiss the little André and Odillon; and see! how sweetly 'Toinette sleeps! All strong and well, son Baptiste! Were one gone, think what thou wouldst have lost! But instead, be thankful, for behold, another has been given, — the little Seraphine here, that thou has not before seen!"

Big, rough, soft-hearted Baptiste knelt by the cradle, and kissed the babe gently.

"It is true, *Memere*," he answered, "and I thank *le bon Dieu* for his goodness to me."

But little Baptiste, lying wide awake for hours afterwards, was not thankful. He could not see that matters could be much worse. A big hard lump was in his throat as he thought of his father's hunger, and the home-coming so different from what they had fondly counted on. Great slow tears came into the boy's eyes, and he wiped them away, ashamed even in the dark to have been guilty of such weakness.

In the gray dawn little Baptiste suddenly awoke, with the sensation of having slept on his post. How heavy his heart was! Why? He sat dazed with indefinite sorrow. Ah, now he remembered! Conolly threatening to turn them out! and his father back penniless! No breakfast! Well, we must see about that.

Very quietly he rose, put on his patched clothes, and went out. Heavy mist covered the face of the river, and somehow the rapid seemed stilled to a deep, pervasive murmur. As he pushed his boat off, the morning fog was chillier than frost about him; but his heart got lighter as he rowed toward his night-line, and he became even eager for the pleasure of handling his fish. He made up his mind not to be much disappointed if there were no sturgeon, but could not quite believe there would be none; surely it was reasonable to expect *one*, perhaps two — why not three? — among the catfish and *doré*.

How very taut and heavy the rope felt as he raised it over his gunwales, and letting the bow swing upstream, began pulling in the line hand over hand! He had heard of cases where every hook had its fish; such a thing might happen again surely! Yard after yard of rope he passed slowly over the boat, and down into the water it sank on his track.

Now a knot on the line told him he was nearing the first hook; he watched for the quiver and struggle of the fish, — probably a big one, for there he had put a tremendous bait on and spat on it for luck, moreover. What? the short line hung down from the rope, and the baited hook rose clear of the water!

Baptiste instantly made up his mind that that hook had been placed a little too far inshore; he remembered thinking so before; the next hook was in about the right place!

Hand over hand, ah! the second hook, too! Still baited, the big worm very livid! It must be thus because that worm was pushed up the shank of the hook in such a queer way: he had been rather pleased when he gave the bait that particular twist, and now was surprised at himself; why, any one could see it was a thing to scare fish!

Hand over hand to the third, — the hook was naked of bait! Well, that was more satisfactory; it showed they had been biting, and after all, this was just about the beginning of the right place.

Hand over hand; *now* the splashing will begin, thought little Baptiste, and out came the fourth hook with its livid worm! He held the rope in his hand without drawing it in for a few moments, but could see no reasonable objection to that last worm. His heart sank a little, but pshaw! only four hooks out of forty were up yet! wait till the eddy behind the shoal was reached, then great things would be seen. Maybe the fish had not been lying in that first bit of current.

Hand over hand again, now! yes, certainly, *there* is the right swirl! What? a *losch*, that unclean semi-lizard! The boy tore it off and flung it indignantly into the river. However, there was good luck in a *losch*; that was well known.

But the next hook, and the next, and next, and next came up baited and fishless. He pulled hand over hand quickly — not a fish! and he must have gone over half the line! Little Baptiste stopped, with his heart like lead and his arms trembling. It was terrible! Not a fish, and his father had no supper, and there was no credit at the store. Poor little Baptiste!

Again he hauled hand over hand — one hook, two, three — oh! ho! Glorious! What a delightful sheer downward the rope took! Surely the big sturgeon at last, trying to stay down on the bottom with the hook! But Baptiste would show that fish his mistake. He pulled, pulled, stood up to pull; there was a sort of shake, a sudden give of the rope, and little Baptiste tumbled over backward as he jerked his line up from under the big stone!

Then he heard the shutters clattering as Conolly's clerk took them off the store window; at half-past five to the minute that was always done. Soon big Baptiste would be up, that

was certain. Again the boy began hauling in line: baited hook! baited hook! naked hook! baited hook! — such was still the tale.

"Surely, surely," implored little Baptiste, silently, "I shall find some fish!" Up! up! only four remained! The boy broke down. Could it be? Had he not somehow skipped many hooks? Could it be that there was to be no breakfast for the children? Naked hook again! Oh, for some fish! anything! three, two!

"Oh, send just one for my father! — my poor, hungry father!" cried little Baptiste, and drew up his last hook. It came full baited, and the line was out of the water clear away to his outer buoy!

He let go the rope and drifted down the river, crying as though his heart would break. All the good hooks useless! all the labor thrown away! all his self-confidence come to naught!

Up rose the great sun; from around the kneeling boy drifted the last of the morning mists; bright beams touched his bowed head tenderly. He lifted his face and looked up the rapid. Then he jumped to his feet with sudden wonder; a great joy lit up his countenance.

Far up the river a low, broad, white patch appeared on the sharp sky-line made by the level dark summit of the long slope of tumbling water. On this white patch stood many figures of swaying men black against the clear morning sky, and little Baptiste saw instantly that an attempt was being made to "run" a "band" of deals, or many cribs lashed together, instead of single cribs as had been done the day before.

The broad strip of white changed its form slowly, dipped over the slope, drew out like a wide ribbon, and soon showed a distinct slant across the mighty volume of the deep raft channel. When little Baptiste, acquainted as he was with every current, eddy, and shoal in the rapid, saw that slant, he knew that his first impression of what was about to happen had been correct. The pilot of the band *had* allowed it to drift too far north before reaching the rapid's head.

Now the front cribs, instead of following the curve of the channel, had taken slower water, while the rear cribs, impelled by the rush under them, swung the band slowly across the current. All along the front the standing men swayed back and forth, plying sweeps full forty feet long, attempting to swing into channel again, with their strokes dashing the dark rollers before the band into wide splashes of white. On the rear cribs another crew pulled in the contrary direction; about the middle of the band stood the pilot, urging his gangs with gestures to greater efforts.

Suddenly he made a new motion; the gang behind drew in their oars and ran hastily forward to double the force in front. But they came too late! Hardly had the doubled bow crew taken a stroke when all drew in their oars and ran back to be out of danger. Next moment the front cribs struck the "hog's back" shoal.

Then the long broad band curved downward in the center, the rear cribs swung into the shallows on the opposite side of the raft-channel, there was a great straining and crashing, the men in front huddled together, watching the wreck anxiously, and the band went speedily to pieces. Soon a fringe of single planks came downstream, then cribs and pieces of cribs; half the band was drifting with the currents, and half was "hung up" on the rocks among the breakers.

Launching the big red flat-bottomed bow boat, twenty of the raftsmen came with wild speed down the river, and as there had been no rush to get aboard, little Baptiste knew that the cribs on which the men stood were so hard aground that no lives were in danger. It meant much to him; it meant that he was instantly at liberty to gather in *money!* money, in sums that loomed to gigantic figures before his imagination.

He knew that there was an important reason for hurrying the deals to Quebec, else the great risk of running a band at that season would not have been undertaken; and he knew that hard cash would be paid down as salvage for all planks brought ashore, and thus secured from drifting far and wide over the lake-like expanse below the rapid's foot. Little Baptiste plunged his oars in and made for a clump of deals floating in the eddy near his own shore. As he rushed along, the raftsmen's boat crossed his bows, going to the main raft below for ropes and material to secure the cribs coming down intact.

"Good boy!" shouted the foreman to Baptiste, "Ten cents for every deal you fetch ashore above the raft!"

Ten cents! he had expected but five! What a harvest!

Striking his pike-pole into the clump of deals, — "fifty at least", said joyful Baptiste, — he soon secured them to his boat, and then pulled, pulled, pulled, till the blood rushed to his head, and his arms ached, before he landed his wealth.

"Father!" cried he, bursting breathlessly into the sleeping household. "Come quick! I can't get it up without you."

"Big sturgeon?" cried the shantyman, jumping into his trousers.

"Oh, but we shall have a good fish breakfast!" cried Delima.

"Did I not say the blessed *le bon Dieu* would send plenty fish?" observed *Memere*.

"Not a fish!" cried little Baptiste, with recovered breath.

"But look! look!" and he flung open the door. The eddy was now white with planks.

"Ten cents for each!" cried the boy. "The foreman told me."

"Ten cents!" shouted his father. "*Baptême!* it's my winter's wages!"

And the old grandmother! And Delima? Why, they just put their arms round each other and cried for joy.

"And yet there's no breakfast," said Delima, starting up. "And they will work hard, hard."

At that instant who should reach the door but Monsieur Conolly! He was a man who respected cash wherever he found it, and already the two Baptistes had a fine show ashore.

"Ma'ame Larocque," said Conolly, politely, putting in his head, "of course you know I was only joking yesterday. You can get anything you want at the store."

What a breakfast they did have, to be sure! the Baptistes eating while they worked. Back and forward they dashed till late afternoon, driving ringed spikes into the deals, running light ropes through the rings, and, when a good string had thus been made, going ashore to haul in. At that hauling Delima and *Memere*, even little André and Odillon gave a hand.

Everybody in the little hamlet made money that day, but the Larocques twice as much as any other family, because they had an eddy and a low shore. With the help of the people "the big *Bourgeois*" who owned the broken raft got it away that evening, and saved his fat contract after all.

"Did I not say so?" said *Memere*, at night for the hundredth time. "Did I not say so? Yes, indeed, *le bon Dieu* watches over us all."

132   E. W. Thomson

"Yes, indeed, grandmother," echoed little Baptiste, thinking of his failure on the night-line. "We may take as much trouble as we like, but it's no use unless *le bon Dieu* helps us. Only I don't know what de big Bourgeois say about that, his raft was all broke up so bad."

"Ah, *oui*," said *Memere*, looking puzzled for but a moment. "But he didn't put his trust in *le bon Dieu*; that's it, for sure. Besides, maybe *le bon Dieu* want to teach him a lesson; he'll not try for run a whole band of deals next time. You see that was a tempting of Providence; and then — the big Bourgeois is a Protestant."

Series Jitters

Leslie McFarlane

When Amby Porter, manager-coach of the Blues, brought his own son up from the farm club and threw him into the fifth game of the finals, already tied at two games apiece, he knew he was putting himself on the spot.

When he pulled his goalie in the final minute of the game, gambling that his team could tie up the score and go on to win in overtime, he was merely exercising good judgment. The Foxes were fading and his Blues were coming on. It could have worked.

But when young Bud caught the goalie out of position and shot the puck over a wide-open net with ten seconds to go, it was then Bud Porter who was on the spot. Nervous, jittery, over-anxious — the kid blew it.

The fact that he had almost whacked the puck into his own net halfway through the second period didn't help either.

The other players didn't say anything but their faces were grim. The fans had plenty to say. So did the sports writers.

Bud gulped down a sample at breakfast with his father next morning.

Parental pride is all right in its place but Amby Porter should wake up to the fact that it should have no place in the job of masterminding a big league hockey club during series playoff. Son Bud is a promising player who will go far in the game — but he hasn't gone far enough yet. That missed goal might well have been the turning point of the entire series. Around the Blue camp it is an open secret that as the series goes, so goes Amby Porter's chances for a renewal of contract.

Amby Porter was drinking coffee with a preoccupied air, but he didn't seem worried. It was pretty hard to read Amby Porter's mind.

"Did you see this, dad?"

Bud thrust the folded newspaper across the table, indicating the troublesome paragraph with his finger.

Amby Porter nodded shortly. "I saw it."

"I guess it's true, isn't it?"

"That part about over-anxiety is true enough. Honest, Bud, if you went down to the rink this morning and practised trying to get that puck over the net from that angle and from that close in, I'll bet you couldn't do it — not if you tried for an hour."

Bud sat back in his chair. "I guess you'd better drop me, and bring up one of the other fellows," he said.

Amby Porter took another sip of coffee. "If you'd scored that goal, the reporters would have been on the other side of the fence, cheering their heads off for you. That shot was close. Even if you weren't my son I'd have picked you from the farm team."

"You would?"

"Think I'm so dumb that I'd have thrown you into the series if you weren't good enough? Huh! I may be sentimental, but I'm not *that* sentimental."

"Yes, but I'm not good enough," insisted Bud stubbornly. "I get out there and I seem to forget all the hockey I ever learned."

"I know what's wrong with you."

"I'm too young."

"Get that idea out of your head. I can name you a score of stars who were topnotch players at twenty-one. You've got natural ability. You can skate, stick-handle, shoot and pass. You've got hockey instinct. Your legs will never be better — one reason I brought you up. Older players have to save their legs. You don't tire now."

"If I'm as good as all that," said Bud bitterly, "we wouldn't have lost that game last night."

"You didn't lose it. Our defense let in three goals. Our forwards couldn't get more than two. You might have helped win it, I'll admit that. You didn't play the sort of hockey you can play, I'll tell you that. Because you've had a fine case of the S. J.'s ever since you got into the series."

"What are the S. J.'s?"

"Series Jitters. That's what you've got. And you'd better shake them off."

"You mean I've got stage fright?"

"Stage fright or ice fright or whatever you want to call it. I've seen a veteran of twelve seasons come down with it. Pressure. You think the whole weight of the hockey world is on your shoulders and it's too much for you."

Bud knew Amby Porter had put his finger right on the trouble.

"What's the cure?" he asked his father.

"Stop reading the papers, for one thing," bellowed Amby Porter suddenly. He snatched up the offending sheet from the table and hurled it into a corner.

"Yes, but — "

"Stop reading the papers. Don't listen to one solitary sports commentator until this is over. Don't listen to a hockey fan. Don't talk hockey at all. And when you get out there in the next game — "

"You're going to use me?"

"I figure my judgment of hockey players is still pretty good, no matter how many sports writers think they could do better. You're in there until you prove me wrong."

Amby Porter got up and strode out of the room. Bud stared at his plate. For all his father's contempt for the sports writers, Bud knew there was plenty of truth in what he had just read. And the most uncomfortable truth of all was in the last line.

As the series went, so went Amby Porter's chances for a renewal of his contract as manager of the Blues.

The Blues went into the sixth game fighting mad. They snagged a goal for themselves in the first five minutes of play, to the delirious joy of a hockey-wild crowd, and then settled down to the grim business of protecting their slim lead, with the hope of extending it on breakaways.

"Remember what I told you," Amby Porter said to his son the first time he sent Bud out. "Keep your head up and do your best. If we win, you won't deserve the credit, and if we lose, you won't deserve the blame."

Bud tried to forget that he was playing for a championship. He went out and backchecked.

They struggled through the second period, hanging on to that one-goal lead. They went into the third and the Foxes opened up more and more.

They came into the stretch, down into the last ten minutes, the last five, the last three. Manager Amby Porter sat up a little straighter on the bench. His face was like rock. He was quivering with suspense but his expression didn't show it. There was an offside at the Blues' line.

"All right," said Amby Porter huskily, as he sent out reserves. "Hold them."

Bud, rested after six minutes on the bench, swooped over to his spot on the wing. For the first time that night, he was quaking. Three minutes away from tying up the series again. The Foxes would shoot the works. Hold them out for three minutes. Three minutes!

The Blues faltered. Their goalie had to make half a dozen quick saves. Bud, hanging on to Renault, saw that the defense was crumbling. The puck went flying into a corner and he chased Renault after it.

Renault tried to hoist him into the boards, but he dodged and collared the puck. Renault crowded him, hacking at his stick. Bud heard a stick rap sharply on the ice, just a few feet away. Harried by Renault, he threw a blind pass.

Then he looked up. Bradley, the Fox center, had the disk on the end of his stick, in the clear and right at the net. Bradley took one stride and fired. The puck plunked into the net.

Bud Porter had fallen for the oldest gag in hockey — the faked pass signal — and the Foxes had tied the score.

The resentful roar of the crowd came rumbling down from the farthest rows. Aghast, Bud stood staring at the Blue goalie, who was sprawled on the ice and gazing up at him with the incredulous expression of one who has been double-crossed by his best friend.

Amby Porter didn't use his son again that night. He didn't dare. Bud had gone to pieces. The Blues squeezed out their win finally, but it took eighteen minutes of the toughest and costliest sort of overtime before they got the extra goal.

Costly because Heffernan, center, was carried off the ice with a skate gash in his leg.

The Blues had won, the series would go the limit, but Amby Porter was fuming when the team straggled back into the dressing room.

Newspapermen were now crowding into the dressing room. They surrounded Amby Porter. "What have you got to say, Amby?" one of them asked.

The old-timer shrugged. "Usual stuff. It was a tough game, but we won on our merits, and now that the chips are down, I'm confident my men are good enough to take them on their own ice."

"But you didn't have much luck during the regular playing schedule," objected one. "They only lost one game to you on their own ice during the season."

"That was schedule hockey," said Amby brusquely. "This is something else again."

"Planning any changes?"

"I've got to bring up a player to replace Heffernan. Have to juggle my lines a little. Losing him is a tough break."

One of the sports writers looked Amby in the eye. "Using Bud in the final game?"

Amby gave him the look right back. "Why not?"

"We've got a statement from one of the club directors. He says he thinks you're playing favorites. Says the kid played a terrible game and that if you lose the series, he'll never vote to renew your contract next year."

"That's one man's opinion," snapped Amby Porter. "But I'm still managing this team, and if I use Bud in Thursday night's game, it will be because I think he can play hockey, not because he's my son. He made a bad pass tonight. So what? Did you see any other bad passes made during that game?"

"Several, but they didn't cost goals."

"It was just Bud's tough luck that his bad pass did cost a goal. But let me say this: the Foxes are a strong team. On tonight's play, they deserved at least one goal. A shut-out wouldn't have given the true measure of that outfit, and you can quote me as saying that."

Amby Porter knew something about pre-game pressure.

But when he came into the dressing room the next evening and took a look at Bud, his heart sank. Bud's mouth was tense and drawn; there were little telltale signs of nerves strung to the snapping point.

"How do you feel?" asked Amby quietly.

"Fine."

"That's good. I just had a talk with Pennell."

Pennell was the club president.

Bud looked up quickly. "About your contract?"

Amby Porter grinned. He slapped Bud's knee. "Everything's going to be all right, no matter how this game comes out."

That took a weight off Bud's mind. The Blues might lose the Cup, but at least his father wouldn't lose his job on that account. Bud felt so light-hearted when he was sent out at the six-minute mark that he found himself playing without strain, playing cool, heads-up hockey, as if this was no different from a hundred other games.

The Foxes nicked the first goal at seventeen minutes, but the Blues countered thirty seconds later when they waltzed through with a swift triple-passing play. The teams went into the second period on even terms.

The game got rough.

Midway in the second period the players began to crack under the pressure of hard going and a tied score in a tied series. Sticks were carried high. It exploded in a grand free-for-all down behind the Fox net when a Fox goalie tripped a forward streaking past the net.

Bud stayed out of it as the referee sorted out the combatants and began dealing out penalties. He leaned up against the boards.

"I wouldn't like to be in Amby Porter's shoes right now," he heard a man in a rinkside seat saying. "This game is too close for comfort."

"Oh, I guess he can take it if the team loses," returned the man in the next seat.

"I was talking to a friend of mine in the press box between periods. He says Pennell told Amby Porter that it was win or else — "

"Else what?"

"Else the Blues have a new manager next year. That's official."

Bud stiffened. *"Everything's going to be all right, no matter how this game comes out."*

That was what Amby Porter had said, but it didn't mean what Bud thought it meant. All it meant was that Amby Porter was trying to put him easy in his mind, trying to ease the strain and pressure. Bud was taut when the teams squared away again, the Blues with a man in the penalty box, but the Foxes two players short.

Struggling with Renault behind the blue line a few moments later, he wrenched himself clear just in time to see the puck come skipping across the ice, right to his stick. Bud slashed at it frantically, sent it skimming and bouncing far down the ice.

He felt sick when he looked up and saw that the Foxes didn't have a man back. He had been in the clear for a breakaway and a clear road to the goal, and didn't know it.

Bud caught his father's eye. Amby Porter made a curt gesture. Bud skated to the gate as a substitute scrambled out to take his place.

Amby Porter never gave pep talks. In the rest session between periods he simply said to the team:

"You've had a long season. You look pretty tired and bunged up. You've played good hockey all through and tonight you've played fantastic hockey. You're going to win, because you're the best team. So get this last twenty minutes over with, and then we'll forget about hockey until next fall."

Bud had no hope that he would be used in the last period at all. But promptly at the six-minute mark when lines were changed, Amby Porter sent him out as usual.

The score was still tied. Bud would have been willing to trade in five years of his life for that extra goal, and he went after it like a madman. Anything to show the world that Amby Porter had been right.

Bud snatched up a pass at center ice, shook off Renault, tore across the blue line, and tried to crash the defense single-handed. The result was that he got tossed on his ear, and the Foxes broke away on a rush that almost sent the red light flickering.

Bud skated back like mad. There was only a single thought in his mind — to get that goal if he had to skate himself into exhaustion doing it.

Bud charged in again, saw a defenseman loom up ahead just as the loose puck rolled out. He lunged for it and pushed the puck into a wild pile-up of players just outside the crease. And then the defenseman hit him.

Bud had a clear glimpse of the goal light gleaming behind

the back screen as he pitched head foremost against the goal post. Then there was a violent, stunning shock, and blackness.

"The crazy kid!" howled Amby Porter. "He'll be lucky if he didn't break his neck." And then Amby let up a louder howl than ever. For the referee was shaking his head; the goalie had the puck wedged tightly between skate and post, right on the line. The score was still tied.

Bud opened his eyes and blinked in the dressing room light. Jimmy Hales, the trainer, was sponging his face. Bud sat up, groggily, gave his head a shake and slipped unsteadily down from the table.

"I've got to get out there, Jimmy," he mumbled. "They're still playing, aren't they?"

"Five minutes to go," grunted Jimmy Hales. "You got a bump on your head as big as an egg. Better stay here."

"Stay here while the game is still on?" yelled Bud. "Where's my stick?"

The trainer was just as glad. He wanted to see that last five minutes himself, even if the Blues were two goals down by now. And although he knew Bud would have a rousing headache before long, his skull was still in one piece.

Bud cast a hurried glance at the clock as he reached the bench and sat down beside Amby Porter.

"Five minutes. And we're two goals up!" he gloated, seeing the big "three" and "one" above and beneath the clock. "We're in!"

Amby Porter's mouth opened. He was just about to growl, "You're reading those figures wrong, son," when he decided to hold his tongue.

"Go out on the next change," he said.

Thirty seconds later, at the next offside, Bud was off the bench before the referee's whistle had stopped blowing. Three to one, he was thinking. Two goals up. The Foxes would never make that up.

Amby Porter's job was safe for another year. That cloud wasn't hanging over his head any more. Of course, if there was a chance to grab another goal just for good measure —

The chance came. It came before he had been out there two minutes. A long forward pass that he reached just at the blue line, a pass to center, a wide shot.

Bud went in after the rebound. Not in a wild frenzy, as if the fate of nations depended on it. After all, they were two goals up. But swiftly, neatly, hooking it away from a defenseman who tried to give him the hip.

Bud took his time, flipped the puck over. Harris, at full momentum, picked it up and let fly. A masked shot, with his own center ahead of him. A back-hander that no goalie could have blocked.

The puck whipped into the net. And this time the referee didn't shake his head.

The Foxes, seeing their lead whittled down to one lone goal, were shaken. They packed their defense, which puzzled Bud Porter mightily. It should be the other way around, but he didn't have much time to think about it in the wild struggle that ensued at the Fox line.

Coolly, he picked up a pass and blistered a shot that just skimmed outside the post. A Fox defenseman charged him, stick high, and he went into the boards with a crash. The whistle shrilled. The defenseman was thumbed to the penalty box.

Bud picked himself up, groggy all over again, and a substitute tapped him. "I'm taking over, Bud."

Bud skated to the bench. He managed a grin as he came in.

"Three goals up and three minutes to go, dad," he chirped. "They won't catch us now."

"Three goals up, my neck!" bawled Amby Porter, leaping up and down in his excitement. "We're within a goal of tying the score, and we've got the odd man! We've got a chance now! A chance!"

Bud sagged. He flopped to the bench. He stared at the clock again and blinked. Visitors' score in the lower slot, hometeam score in the upper. But the Blues were the visitors this time.

Then the jitters swept all over him again, as he watched his team mates pitch into the faltering, short-handed Foxes. And they were swept away in a wild rush of insane delight when the power play cracked the Fox defense, and a Blue forward tricked his way into the clear, picked up a short pass and banged it home over a prostrate goalie.

A two-goal lead wiped out in as many minutes, and a man in the penalty box. The tiring Foxes broke. They broke wide open. Even the return of their penalized player didn't save them. The Blues were climbing, and the Foxes were on the way out.

At nineteen minutes, the Blue center swooped around the back of the net and hooked the puck around the goal post for the tie breaker.

Amby Porter tossed his son a folded newspaper at breakfast on the plane the next morning. "Read that," he said with a grin.

Bud didn't read more than a few lines.

Undoubtedly the turning point of the game was Bud

Porter's surprise assist which put the Blues back into the fight when they seemed thoroughly beaten. Porter, whose inexperience had made him the weak member of the outfit earlier in the series, redeemed himself by the finest play of the night when he picked his way out of a corner and laid down a perfect pass to Harris, who whipped in the goal that sent the Blues on their way —

Bud reached for the coffee. "Yeah, I'm a fine player," he said. "Just give me a two-goal lead and I'm not afraid of anybody."

"Just let anybody try to tell me I can't pick hockey players," beamed Amby Porter. "Now that you've got those jitters out of your system — next season we'll show them!"

Buggam Grange:
A Good Old Ghost Story

Stephen Leacock

The evening was already falling as the vehicle in which I was contained entered upon the long and gloomy avenue that leads to Buggam Grange. A resounding shriek echoed through the wood as I entered the avenue. I paid no attention to it at the moment, judging it to be merely one of those resounding shrieks which one might expect to hear in such a place at such a time. As my drive continued, however, I found myself wondering in spite of myself why such a shriek should have been uttered at the very moment of my approach.

I am not by temperament in any degree a nervous man, and yet there was much in my surroundings to justify a certain feeling of apprehension. The Grange is situated in the loneliest part of England, the marsh country of the fens to which civilization has still hardly penetrated. The inhabitants, of whom there are only one and a half to the square mile, live here and there among the fens and eke out a miserable existence by frog fishing and catching flies. They speak a dialect so broken as to be practically unintelligible, while the perpetual rain which falls upon them renders speech itself almost superfluous.

Here and there where the ground rises slightly above the level of the fens there are dense woods tangled with parasitic creepers and filled with owls. Bats fly from wood to wood.

The air on the lower ground is charged with the poisonous gases which exude from the marsh, while in the woods it is heavy with the dank odors of deadly nightshade and poison ivy.

It had been raining in the afternoon, and as I drove up the avenue the mournful dripping of the rain from the dark trees accentuated the cheerlessness of the gloom. The vehicle in which I rode was a fly on three wheels, the fourth having apparently been broken and taken off, causing the fly to sag on one side and drag on its axle over the muddy ground, the fly thus moving only at a foot's pace in a way calculated to enhance the dreariness of the occasion. The driver on the box in front of me was so thickly muffled up as to be indistinguishable, while the horse which drew us was so thickly coated with mist as to be practically invisible. Seldom, I may say, have I had a drive of so mournful a character.

The avenue presently opened out upon a lawn with overgrown shrubberies and in the half darkness I could see the outline of the Grange itself, a rambling, dilapidated building. A dim light struggled through the casement of a window in a tower room. Save for the melancholy cry of a row of owls sitting on the roof, and croaking of the frogs in the moat which ran around the grounds, the place was soundless. My driver halted his horse at the hither side of the moat. I tried in vain to urge him, by signs, to go further. I could see by the fellow's face that he was in a paroxysm of fear and indeed nothing but the extra sixpence which I had added to his fare would have made him undertake the drive up the avenue. I had no sooner alighted than he wheeled his cab about and made off.

Laughing heartily at the fellow's trepidation (I have a way of laughing heartily in the dark), I made my way to the door

and pulled the bell-handle. I could hear the muffled reverbera-
tions of the bell far within the building. Then all was silent. I
bent my ear to listen, but could hear nothing except perhaps
the sound of a low moaning as of a person in pain or in great
mental distress. Convinced, however, from what my friend
Sir Jeremy Buggam had told me, that the Grange was not
empty, I raised the ponderous knocker and beat with it loudly
against the door.

But perhaps at this point I may do well to explain to my
readers (before they are too frightened to listen to me) how I
came to be beating on the door of Buggam Grange at nightfall
on a gloomy November evening.

A year before I had been sitting with Sir Jeremy Buggam,
the present baronet, on the verandah of his ranch in Califor-
nia.

"So you don't believe in the supernatural?" he was saying.

"Not in the slightest," I answered, lighting a cigar as I
spoke. When I want to speak very positively, I generally light
a cigar as I speak.

"Well, at any rate, Digby," said Sir Jeremy, "Buggam
Grange is haunted. If you want to be assured of it go down
there any time and spend the night and you'll see for yourself."

"My dear fellow," I replied, "nothing will give me greater
pleasure. I shall be back in England in six weeks, and I shall be
delighted to put your ideas to the test. Now tell me," I added
somewhat cynically, "is there any particular season or day
when your Grange is supposed to be specially terrible?"

Sir Jeremy looked at me strangely. "Why do you ask that?"
he said. "Have you heard the story of the Grange?"

"Never heard of the place in my life," I answered cheerily.
"Till you mentioned it tonight, my dear fellow, I hadn't the
remotest idea that you still owned property in England."

"The Grange is shut up," said Sir Jeremy, "and has been for twenty years. But I keep a man there — Horrod — he was butler in my father's time and before. If you care to go, I'll write him that you're coming. And since you are taking your own fate in your hands, the fifteenth of November is the day."

At that moment Lady Buggam and Clara and the other girls came trooping out on the verandah, and the whole thing passed clean out of my mind. Nor did I think of it again until I was back in London. Then by one of those strange coincidences or premonitions — call it what you will — it suddenly occurred to me one morning that it was the fifteenth of November. Whether Sir Jeremy had written to Horrod or not, I did not know. But none the less nightfall found me, as I have described, knocking at the door of Buggam Grange.

The sound of the knocker had scarcely ceased to echo when I heard the shuffling of feet within, and the sound of chains and bolts being withdrawn. The door opened. A man stood before me holding a lighted candle which he shaded with his hand. His faded black clothes, once apparently a butler's dress, his white hair and advanced age left me in no doubt that he was Horrod of whom Sir Jeremy had spoken.

Without a word he motioned me to come in, and, still without speech, he helped me to remove my wet outer garments, and then beckoned me into a great room, evidently the dining room of the Grange.

I am not in any degree a nervous man by temperament, as I think I remarked before, and yet there was something in the vastness of the wainscotted room, lighted only by a single candle, and in the silence of the empty house, and still more in the appearance of my speechless attendant which gave me a feeling of distinct uneasiness. As Horrod moved to and fro I took occasion to scrutinize his face more narrowly. I have

seldom seen features more calculated to inspire a nervous dread. The pallor of his face and the whiteness of his hair (the man was at least seventy), and still more the peculiar furtiveness of his eyes, seemed to mark him as one who lived under a great terror. He moved with a noiseless step and at times he turned his head to glance in the dark corners of the room.

"Sir Jeremy told me," I said, speaking as loudly and as heartily as I could, "that he would apprise you of my coming."

I was looking into his face as I spoke.

In answer Horrod laid his finger across his lips and I knew that he was deaf and dumb. I am not nervous (I think I said that), but the realization that my sole companion in the empty house was a deaf mute struck a cold chill to my heart.

Horrod laid in front of me a cold meat pie, a cold goose, a cheese and a tall flagon of cider. But my appetite was gone. I ate the goose, but found that after I had finished the pie I had but little zest for the cheese, which I finished without enjoyment. The cider had a sour taste, and after having permitted Horrod to refill the flagon twice, I found that it induced a sense of melancholy and decided to drink no more.

My meal finished, the butler picked up the candle and beckoned to me to follow him. We passed through the empty corridors of the house, a long line of pictured Buggams looking upon us as we passed, their portraits in the flickering light of the taper assuming a strange and life-like appearance as if leaning forward from their frames to gaze upon the intruder.

Horrod led me upstairs and I realized that he was taking me to the tower in the east wing in which I had observed a light.

The rooms to which the butler conducted me consisted of a sitting room with an adjoining bedroom, both of them fitted with antique wainscotting against which a faded tapestry fluttered. There was a candle burning on the table in the sitting room but its insufficient light only rendered the surroundings the more dismal. Horrod bent down in front of the fireplace and endeavored to light a fire there. But the wood was evidently damp, and the fire flickered feebly on the hearth.

The butler left me, and in the stillness of the house I could hear his shuffling step echo down the corridor. It may have been fancy, but it seemed to me that his departure was the signal for a low moan that came from somewhere behind the wainscot. There was a narrow cupboard door at one side of the room, and for the moment I wondered whether the moaning came from within. I am not as a rule lacking in courage (I am sure my reader will be decent enough to believe this), yet I found myself entirely unwilling to open the cupboard door and look within. In place of doing so I seated myself in a great chair in front of the feeble fire. I must have been seated there for some time when I happened to lift my eyes to the mantel above and saw, standing upon it, a letter addressed to myself. I knew the handwriting at once to be that of Sir Jeremy Buggam.

I opened it, and spreading it out within reach of the feeble candle light, I read as follows:

My dear Digby,

In our talk you will remember I had no time to finish telling you about the mystery of Buggam Grange. I take for granted, however, that you will go there and that Horrod will put you in the tower rooms, which are the only ones that make any pretense of being habitable. I have, therefore, sent him this letter to deliver at the Grange itself. The story is this:

On the night of the fifteenth of November, fifty years ago, my grandfather was murdered in the room in which you are sitting, by his cousin Sir Duggam Buggam. He was stabbed from behind while seated at the little table at which you are probably reading this letter. The two had been playing cards at the table and my grandfather's body was found lying in a litter of cards and gold sovereigns on the floor. Sir Duggam Buggam, insensible from drink, lay beside him, the fatal knife at his hand, his fingers smeared with blood. My grandfather, though of the younger branch, possessed a part of the estates which were to revert to Sir Duggam on his death. Sir Duggam Buggam was tried at the Assizes and was hanged. On the day of his execution he was permitted by the authorities, out of respect for his rank, to wear a mask to the scaffold. The clothes in which he was executed are hanging at full length in the little cupboard to your right, and the mask is above them. It is said that on every fifteenth of November at midnight the cupboard door opens and Sir Duggam Buggam walks out into the room. It has been found impossible to get servants to remain at the Grange, and the place — except for the presence of Horrod — has been unoccupied for a generation. At the time of the murder Horrod was a young man of twenty-two, newly entered into the service of the family. It was he who entered the room and discovered the crime. On the day of the execution he was stricken with paralysis and has never spoken since. From that time to this he has never consented to leave the Grange where he lives in isolation.

Wishing you a pleasant night after your tiring journey,

> I remain,
> Very faithfully,
> *Jeremy Buggam*

I leave my reader to imagine my state of mind when I completed the perusal of the letter.

I have as little belief in the supernatural as anyone, yet I must confess that there was something in the surroundings in which I now found myself which rendered me at least uncomfortable. My reader may smile if he will, but I assure him that it was with a very distinct feeling of uneasiness that I at length managed to rise to my feet, and, grasping my candle in my hand, to move backward into the bedroom. As I backed into it something so like a moan seemed to proceed from the closed cupboard that I accelerated my backward movement to a considerable degree. I hastily blew out the candle, threw myself upon the bed and drew the bed clothes over my head, keeping, however, one eye and one ear still out and available.

How long I lay thus listening to every sound, I cannot tell. The stillness had become absolute. From time to time I could dimly hear the distant cry of an owl and once far away in the building below a sound as of someone dragging a chain along a floor. More than once I was certain that I heard the sound of moaning behind the wainscot. Meantime I realized that the hour must now be drawing close upon the fatal moment of midnight. My watch I could not see in the darkness, but by reckoning the time that must have elapsed I knew that midnight could not be far away. Then presently my ear, alert to every sound, could just distinguish far away across the fens the striking of a church bell, in the clock tower of Buggam village church, no doubt, tolling the hour of twelve.

On the last stroke of twelve, the cupboard door in the next room opened. There is no need to ask me how I knew it. I couldn't, of course, see it, but I could hear, or sense in some way, the sound of it. I could feel my hair, all of it, rising upon my head. I was aware that there was a *presence* in the adjoining room, I will not say a person, a living soul, but a *presence*. Anyone who has been in the next room to a presence will know just how I felt. I could hear a sound as of someone groping on the floor and the faint rattle as of coins.

My hair was now perpendicular. My reader can blame it or not, but it was.

Then at this very moment from somewhere below in the building there came the sound of a prolonged and piercing cry, a cry as of a soul passing in agony. My reader may censure me or not, but right at this moment I decided to beat it. Whether I should have remained to see what was happening is a question that I will not discuss. My one idea was to get out and to get out quickly. The window of the tower room was some twenty-five feet above the ground. I sprang out through the casement in one leap and landed on the grass below. I jumped over the shrubbery in one bound and cleared the moat in one jump. I went down the avenue in about six strides and ran five miles along the road through the fens in three minutes. This at least is an accurate transcription of my sensations. It may have taken longer. I never stopped till I found myself on the threshold of the Buggam Arms in Little Buggam, beating on the door for the landlord.

I returned to Buggam Grange on the next day in the bright sunlight of a frosty November morning, in a seven cylinder motor car with six local constables and a physician. It makes all the difference. We carried revolvers, spades, pickaxes, shotguns and a ouija board.

What we found cleared up forever the mystery of the Grange. We discovered Horrod the butler lying on the dining room floor quite dead. The physician said that he had died from heart failure. There was evidence from the marks of his shoes in the dust that he had come in the night to the tower room. On the table he had placed a paper which contained a full confession of his having murdered Jeremy Buggam fifty years before. The circumstances of the murder had rendered it easy for him to fasten the crime upon Sir Duggam, already insensible from drink. A few minutes with the ouija board enabled us to get a full corroboration from Sir Duggam. He promised, moreover, now that his name was cleared, to go away from the premises forever.

My friend, the present Sir Jeremy, has rehabilitated Buggam Grange. The place is rebuilt. The moat is drained. The whole house is lit with electricity. There are beautiful motor drives in all directions in the woods. He has had the bats shot and the owls stuffed. His daughter, Clara Buggam, became my wife. She is looking over my shoulder as I write. What more do you want?

The End